Bones

SATAN'S FURY MC- SG

L. WILDER

Bones
Satan's Fury MC
L. Wilder 2023

Without limiting the rights under copyright reserved above, no part of this publication or any part of this series may be reproduced without the prior written permission of both the copyright owner and the above publisher of this book.

This book is a work of fiction. Some of the places named in the book are actual places found in Washington. The names, characters, brands, and incidents are either the product of the author's imagination or are used fictitiously.

The author acknowledges the trademarked status and owners of various products and locations referenced in this work of fiction, which have been used without permission. The publication or use of these trademarks is not authorized, associated with, or sponsored by the trademark owners.

This e-book is licensed for your personal enjoyment only. This e-book may not be re-sold or given away to other people. *All Rights Reserved.*

Book Cover Details:

Photographer: Wander

Model: Brandon

Cover Design: Mayhem Cover Creations

Editor: Marie Peyton

Proofreader: Rose Holub

Personal Assistant: Natalie Weston

Catch up with the entire Satan's Fury MC Series today!

All books are FREE with Kindle Unlimited!

Ties That Bind (Ruthless Sinners #1)

Holding On (Ruthless Sinners #2)

Secrets We Keep (Ruthless Sinners #3)

Widow's Undoing (Ruthless Sinners #4)

Claiming Menace (Ruthless Sinners #5)

Tempting Country (Ruthless Sinners #6)

Jagger's Choice (Ruthless Sinners #7)

Viper's Demands (Ruthless Sinners #8)

Lynch's Rule (Ruthless Sinners #9)

The Butcher (Ruthless Sinners #10)

Summer Storm (Satan's Fury MC Novella)

Maverick (Satan's Fury MC #1)

Stitch (Satan's Fury MC #2)

Cotton (Satan's Fury MC #3)

Clutch (Satan's Fury MC #4)

Smokey (Satan's Fury MC #5)

Big (Satan's Fury #6)

Two Bit (Satan's Fury #7)

Diesel (Satan's Fury #8)

Falling for the President's Daughter (Satan's Fury #9)

Q (Satan's Fury #10)

Blaze (Satan's Fury MC- Memphis Book 1)

Shadow (Satan's Fury MC- Memphis Book 2)

Riggs (Satan's Fury MC- Memphis Book 3)

Murphy (Satan's Fury MC- Memphis Book 4)

Gunner (Satan's Fury MC- Memphis Book 5)

Gus (Satan's Fury MC- Memphis Book 6)

Rider (Satan's Fury MC- Memphis Book 7)

Prospect (Satan's Fury MC- Memphis Book 8)

T-Bone (Satan's Fury MC-Memphis Book 9)

Day Three (What Bad Boys Do Book 1)

Damaged Goods- (The Redemption Series Book 1- Nitro)

Max's Redemption (The Redemption Series Book 2- Max)

Inferno (Devil Chasers #1)

Smolder (Devil Chaser #2)

Ignite (Devil Chasers #3)

Consumed (Devil Chasers #4)

Combust (Devil Chasers #5)

The Long Road Home (Devil Chasers #6)

Naughty or Nice (Mistletoe, Montana Collaboration)

My Temptation (The Happy Endings Collection #1)

Bring the Heat (The Happy Endings Collection #2)

His Promise (The Happy Endings Collection #3)

❦ Created with Vellum

Sign up for L. Wilder's Newsletter: https://lwilderbooks.us18.list-manage.com/subscribe?u=a2c4c211615b2d7b3dd46289a&id=7f8e916141

Social media Links:
Facebook: *https://www.facebook.com/AuthorLeslieWilder*
TikTok:https://www.tiktok.com/@lwilderauthor?lang=en
Twitter: https://twitter.com/wilder_leslie
Instagram: http://instagram.com/LWilderbooks
Amazon: http://www.amazon.com/L-Wilder/e/B00NDKCCMI/
Bookbub: https://www.bookbub.com/authors/l-wilder

Prologue

"What's wrong with you?"
"Why do you gotta be so weird?"
"You've always got your face buried in that damn game."
"You need to get in the real world."
"Why can't you just be normal?"
"Why was I the one who had to get a fucking retard for a kid?"

I didn't just hear the words. I felt them. I believed them. I had no reason not to. My father was the one saying them. He was a man I was supposed to love and trust, but sadly, I didn't. I hated him, and I certainly didn't trust him.

My mother didn't either—at least, not like she did.

There was a time when she loved him and believed that she'd found her Mr. Right. Sadly, when I came along, she discovered she was wrong, and that realization brought on a great deal of guilt. Not just for her, but for me as well. She hated that he wasn't the father she thought he'd be, and I hated that having me as a kid was so fucking terrible that it had turned him into an asshole.

Mom held on for years, praying that eventually things would get better, but they never did. In fact, they only got worse, and when their fights became physical, she had no choice but to file for divorce.

That's when things really took a turn for the worse.

My father's fuse became even shorter, which meant there was even more yelling, name-calling, and manhandling. It seemed he was intent on proving that tough love would turn me into a normal kid. Mom could see the emotional damage he was inflicting and feared he'd take things too far.

And he did.

I can't remember what set him off. I'm sure it had something to do with me spending too much time on my game or the fact that I wouldn't answer when he spoke, but I'll never forget the look of anger and disgust in his eyes when he grabbed me and started yelling at me.

There was a lot of cursing and belittling, typical

bullshit, but this time was different. This time he nearly broke my arm—which was why I ran.

It wasn't an idea I'd come to on my own.

Mom was terrified that dad would take things too far and begged the courts to take away his rights to visitation, but they refused. Knowing there was a good chance that something terrible might happen, Mom suggested that I get away from him if he tried to hurt me and hide out at a nearby diner.

And that's exactly what I did.

I ran with all my might, and when I finally made it to the diner, I found a dark spot next to the parking lot and sat down with my back against the side of the building. I wrapped my arms around my knees and lowered my head, praying it wouldn't be long before my mother found me.

I hadn't been sitting there long when I heard the loud rumble of a motorcycle pulling into the parking lot. The headlights shone bright, casting away the dark shadows of the night sky, but they only lasted for a moment. Soon, the engine died, and silence fell on the parking lot once again.

My heart started to race when I heard a scuffle of rocks, and the sound only grew louder as someone's boots started walking over to me. Seconds later, I heard, "You alright, kid?"

I didn't answer.

I couldn't.

My mind was too busy trying to make sense of the stranger standing before me. He was a big guy, bigger than any man I'd ever been around, and he had a thick, burly beard and countless tattoos. His large stature alone should've been enough to have me trembling in my Nikes.

But I wasn't scared.

Not in the least.

And that intrigued the hell out of me.

I wanted to know more about him. I wanted to know where he was from and what he was doing here at this diner. I wanted to know why he was so big and why he had such a big beard. More than that, I wanted to know why he had come over to check on me.

I don't know how long he stood there studying me with those coal-black eyes, but it seemed like an eternity. He let out a deep breath, and for a moment, I thought he was going to turn and walk away, leaving me alone out there in the dark.

But he didn't.

Instead, he shoved his hands in his pockets and leaned back against the hard brick wall. He didn't say a word. He simply stood there next to me, and I got the feeling he wasn't going anywhere. It was like he had it set in his head that he was going to stay there and watch out for me. We both remained painfully silent as I sat curled up in a ball next to him.

I kept thinking that he'd say or do something, but he never said a word.

And neither did I.

About half an hour in, a car pulled into the lot, shining its bright lights on us. I didn't think much of it until I noticed the man's expression had suddenly changed and had become eerily fierce. It took me a moment, but I soon realized he was staring at my arm. He'd seen the bruises my father had left on me, and he was clearly bothered by them.

I moved my arm to my side and pretended that it wasn't bothering me, but it was clear from his expression that it was bothering him. He took another deep, cleansing breath, then stepped forward and towered over me.

"Look, kid. I'm starving." His voice was low and steady as he continued, "How about we go inside, and I'll buy you a cheeseburger."

I glanced up at him, and I could see that he was being genuinely sincere. For a second, I almost agreed to take him up on his offer, but then I remembered how my mother had told me never to talk to strangers. The memory of her warning had me shaking my head.

"They make really great burgers, kid." Again, his

voice was low and reassuring. "You sure you don't want one?"

"I like chicken nuggets," I answered as I stared down at my shoes.

"They've got chicken nuggets."

I thought for a moment, then finally answered, "Okay."

I stood and brushed the dust and rocks off my backside, then followed the man over to the front door. Once we were inside, I headed to the back of the diner and sat down in one of the corner booths. I rested my elbows on the table, propped my chin in my hands, and watched as he sat down across from me.

He settled back in the booth, then motioned over to the waitress. Once he'd ordered our food, he turned his attention back to me. "You live around here?"

"No," I answered, playing with the paper from my straw.

I folded the paper into several different shapes and then turned my focus to the other items on the table, putting them each in a perfectly straight line. I was taking the salt and pepper shakers in and out of the line when the waitress brought over our food. I dove into my chicken nuggets, and it wasn't long before I started to feel more at ease.

I looked up at the man, staring at his tough

features as I announced, "You've got a bushy beard and lots of tattoos."

"Yeah, I do."

"The internet says that tattoos are a form of self-expression. That each tattoo has an important meaning."

"I'd say that's about right."

"You also drive a Harley Davidson motorcycle."

"You're pretty observant, kid."

I took another bite of my chicken nugget as I told him, "Harley Davidson motorcycles were founded in 1903, and they were first used by police officers in Detroit, Michigan."

This man was big and had a threatening appearance, but I didn't think twice about rattling off all the facts I'd learned about Harleys. It was something I'd never do with my ol' man—at least, not anymore. He had no patience for my lust for information and was quick to tell me so. I had so many things I wanted to share with my father, but I learned it was best to just keep my mouth shut.

It felt good to be able to speak freely, especially with a complete stranger. Not once did I feel like I was weird or there was something wrong with me. I didn't feel like an outcast or something less. I felt like a regular kid sharing something that was important to me with a friend.

I continued to talk to him about various Harleys and the men who first drove them. In between breaths, he ordered me a sundae, then asked, "You gonna tell me why you're hiding out in the parking lot?"

"Momma told me to come here, to the Old Mill Café, if something bad ever happened." I swallowed hard before adding, "It's our secret place."

Before he could respond, the waitress brought over a sundae and placed it on the table. I immediately grabbed my spoon and started to dig in. As I ate, I looked around the room. The diner was quiet, just an elderly couple sitting at one of the front tables. From time to time, the old lady would turn and sneak a peek at us, clearly curious about what was going on with us, but I didn't care.

I was perfectly content sitting there with him. I had a warm feeling in the pit of my stomach as I looked up at him and said, "Thank you. This is good."

"You got a name?"

"It's Wyatt."

"My name's Stitch."

"Your momma named you Stitch?"

"Nah. My mother named me Griffin, but all my brothers in my club call me Stitch."

While he hadn't actually explained why he was given the nickname, I was able to put two and two together on my own. Something bad had happened to him, probably more than once, and it had left him needing stitches. I looked out the window as I confessed, "My momma had to get stitches one time."

I figured he would ask me why, but he didn't. Instead, he considered what I'd said and gave me a slight nod. After several quiet moments, he asked, "You think we should call her? Tell her you're at the special spot?"

"Yeah."

Stitch had just started to reach for his phone when there was a commotion at the front door that caught his attention. His eyes widened, and a strange look crossed his face. I couldn't make out what was being said behind me, but it was clear that something was wrong. Curious, I turned to see what was happening and was both surprised and relieved to see that it was my mother who was causing the disruption.

Her face went pale as soon as she turned to look in our direction. Frozen in her stance, her dark brown eyes slowly drifted over Stitch, and with each second that passed, she appeared more and more frightened. As soon as she reached our booth, she knelt down next to me and placed her hand on my knee.

Even though she tried to hide it, I could tell that she was worried when she whispered, "Hey, Buddy. Are you okay?"

I nodded, then told her, "This is Griffin. He got

me some chicken nuggets, but I'm done now. Can we go home?"

"Hi, Griffin. I'm Wren." She gave him a forced smile, then turned her attention back to me. "Yeah, buddy. We can go. You did a good job getting here. I'm so proud of you."

"I went down Tucker Street and turned right on Main," I replied proudly. "Just like you showed me."

"You are such a smart boy." She brushed my long hair out of my eyes, then looked back over to Stitch as she explained, "I know this looks bad... really bad, but I'm doing the best I can. I'd tell you what this was all about, but it would take a lifetime to explain. Right now, I need to get him home. How much do I owe you for the food?"

"Don't worry about it. I got it," Stitch told her.

"Thank you so much for looking out for him."

Without giving Stitch a chance to respond, she took me by the hand and helped me out of the booth. Stitch stood up along with me, but he didn't follow us as we started towards the front door. We were just about to go outside when Mom stopped and rushed back over to Stitch. She reached for his hand and whispered something I couldn't make out.

Moments later, she made her way back over to me, and we left.

. . .

I thought that would be the last time I saw Stitch.

It wasn't.

Our brief encounter was the first of many to come.

Over the next twenty years, Stitch and his brothers became an integral part of my life—my mother's, too. They showed us both what it was to truly trust and to love unconditionally, and by doing so, they helped mold me into the man I am today.

CHAPTER 1

Elsie

In just one moment—one thoughtless, irrevocable moment, my entire world was turned inside out. It should've been the end of my story, but thanks to the brothers of Satan's Fury, it was just the beginning.

My life had never been what you'd call easy. It seemed I was always fighting an uphill battle of some kind, but one way or another, I'd always found a way to manage. It was a talent I'd acquired from my parents. Neither of them had a college education, but they'd worked hard to provide a good life for my brother and me.

My dad was a longshoreman and worked countless hours loading and unloading the ships that came into the port. He did fairly well for himself and tried to convince Mom that she didn't need to work, but she never listened. In fact, she often cleaned three or more houses a day just to make sure they had enough to cover the bills and put money into savings.

Together, they gave Brantley and me everything we could want and more. I couldn't imagine things being better, and then, everything fell apart.

My brother had just turned fourteen when they discovered he had a life-threatening brain tumor. Even though they didn't have good insurance, they refused to let that stop them from getting him the best care and took him to every specialist they could find. The bills started piling up, and it wasn't long before they'd drained their entire savings and were living solely on credit.

Even after everything they'd done, my brother was only getting worse.

The tumor continued to grow, and after months of praying and hoping, it finally took my sweet brother's life—leaving my parents with no son and a mountain of bills we couldn't pay.

My parents were devastated. Mom sank into a deep depression and could barely manage to work, cutting back to one house a day and sometimes none at all. Meanwhile, my father had struggles of his own. He went to work every day, but he was a shell of the man he once was. His smile and bubbly personality had all but disappeared.

I wasn't handling Brantley's death any better than my parents. I adored my brother, and it nearly killed me to lose him. While I wanted to crawl into a dark hole and die right along with him, I could never do that to my parents. They needed me, and I intended to do what I could to be there for them the way they'd always been there for me.

Money was tight, especially with Mom cutting back on her houses, so I got a job at a nearby movie theatre. I figured I could help out with the bills and, hopefully, alleviate some of their stress, but the bills just kept rolling in. Even after selling off most of our belongings, we were barely able to keep the lights on.

But we kept trudging along.

Day by day.

Month by month.

And just when we were getting back on our feet, tragedy struck once again.

I'd come home from working the late shift at the theatre and found them sitting side by side on the sofa, nestled beneath my mother's favorite blanket. At first, it looked as though they were both sleeping, but something didn't feel right. Neither of them were sound sleepers and always woke the moment I entered the room, but they both remained eerily quiet.

I walked over to the sofa and gave my mother a gentle nudge as I whispered, "Hey, Mom, I'm home."

She didn't move, so I shook her again—harder this time. "Mom! Wake up!"

Again, she didn't budge. Frantic, I turned my attention to my father and gave him a firm shake as I cried, "Dad! Please wake up! Dad!"

I called 911, then immediately went back to shaking and pleading with them hysterically. Neither of them responded. I couldn't understand what was happening and started searching for some kind of injury but found nothing. As I continued to try to wake them, my head began to pound, and I started to feel dizzy. Suddenly, I felt the heat of Dad's space heater radiating against my ankles.

That's when it hit me.

It was carbon monoxide poisoning. I quickly unplugged the heater, then rushed around and opened all the windows, praying it would be enough to bring them back.

It wasn't.

When the ambulance finally arrived, the medics rushed inside the house and started asking numerous questions, some of which left me feeling like I was at fault for what had happened. I answered them the best I could, then stepped back and let them try to help my parents.

I felt like I was in a nightmare, unable to move or speak. I just stood there, watching as they started doing chest compressions, breathing into their mouths, and using a defibrillator. I could hear the beeping of the machines and the paramedics shouting instructions to each other.

The minutes felt like hours as I watched them work. I wanted to help, but I was too scared to move. I just stood there, praying that they would be able to save my parents. Finally, after what felt like an eternity, one of the paramedics looked up at me and said, "I'm sorry."

My heart sank as I listened to his partner say, "They were too far gone... There's nothing more we can do."

With that, they loaded each of them onto a gurney and covered them with a white sheet. Seconds later, they ushered their lifeless bodies out to the ambulance and closed the door. Before pulling away, one of the medics came over to me and asked, "You got someplace to go?"

"What?" I muttered.

"A place to go?" He glanced back at the ambulance as he said, "The cops will be here any minute. They're gonna have questions, and one of them is gonna be whether or not you have a place to go."

"I don't know."

"I know this is tough. I'm sure you weren't expecting something like this to happen to your folks."

Fighting back my tears, I replied, "No, I wasn't."

"You eighteen?"

"No, but I will be in a few months."

"You got someplace you can stay until then?" When I didn't immediately answer, he pushed, "A grandmother or aunt and uncle?"

"I don't know."

"Well, you best think of something." Concern marked his face as he told me, "Cause if you don't have a place, they'll find you one. And trust me... You don't want that."

Before I could respond, a cop car pulled into the drive. He gave me a quick nod, then whispered, "Good luck."

It was like a nightmare that I couldn't wake up from.

The pain was so unbearable I thought I would actually die from it. I'd never felt so lost or alone and had no idea what I was going to do without them. But I had to figure it out, and I had to figure it out fast. The paramedic was right about the police. They had all kinds of questions and were about to call in a social worker when I lied and told them I could stay with my grandmother.

I knew it was only a temporary fix, but it gave me a chance to forge a plan.

The policemen made their report, then waited as I

went inside and packed a bag. They wanted to drive me over to my grandmother's, but thankfully, I was able to convince them that I could get there on my own.

Over the next few weeks, I kept my head low and tried to stay off anyone's radar. I took what I could from the house, then spent the next couple of months living out of my car. It wasn't ideal, but I was able to manage—until I lost my job at the theatre. With no money coming in, I was in a mess, especially with winter rolling in. I struggled to eat, much less keep gas in my car.

When things got really bad, I started searching dumpsters. Sometimes, I found things I could sell or a bit to eat that got me through a tough spot. I got pretty good at it and could get in and out without anyone spotting me, but one night, I got careless.

I was cold and hungry, so I decided to drive out to Danvers Bar and Grill. I figured they'd have something that might tide me over until morning. Like many times before, I pulled my car around back and waited until the coast was clear, then I hopped out and rushed over to the side door of the dumpster. I was digging deep, looking for anything that didn't look like absolute mush, when I heard a couple of men talking in the distance.

At first, I ignored them and kept digging. But then, the voices got closer, and I realized they were talking about me. I quickly stepped away from the dumpster and started towards my car. I didn't get far before one of them asked, "Hey, kid. You alright?"

"Yeah, I'm good."

"You sure about that? 'Cause it doesn't look that way."

I turned, and my blood ran cold when I got a good look at the two men walking in my direction. They were both massive with beards and tattoos, and they had these fierce expressions that made them look intimidating as hell. I was terrified to be out there alone in the dark with them, but I did my best to hide my fear as I answered, "Yeah, I'm fine. I was... ah, just looking for my keys."

"Is that right?" I could tell by the look on his face he didn't believe me, but he didn't push. Instead, he asked, "You got a name?"

"Yeah, I'm um... Sabrina."

"Sabrina, huh?" Again, it was clear he knew I was lying, but he didn't call me on it. I hoped he would just let it go, but no such luck. "Your folks around?"

"Yeah, they're at home."

"So, if we were to take you home..."

If they went to my house, they'd find the front door covered in yellow safety tape and a completely barren house. My breath caught at the thought, and before I realized what I was saying, I told them, "You can't do that."

"Oh, yeah? Why not?"

"Because they're..." my voice trailed off. "You just can't."

"That's what I thought. You got any idea where they are?"

"Look, I'm sorry if I did something wrong here. Like I said, I was just looking for my keys. I didn't mean any harm."

"You're not in any trouble, kid," he tried to reassure me. "We're just trying to make sure you're okay."

"I told you. I'm fine."

"Yeah, you did." He glanced over at his friend, and then they both turned their attention back to me. "But I'm not buying it."

I needed these guys to stop pushing, so I shrugged and sassed, "Sounds like a personal problem to me."

"We're just trying to help," his friend replied with a strained voice.

"I didn't ask for your help."

"No, you didn't. But I've been in your shoes. I know how hard it can be."

"You don't know anything about me or what I've been through!" I appreciated the fact that they were trying to help, but I was proud and scared. I feared their kind of help would have me tossed into foster care, and I'd spent the last six months doing everything I could to make sure that didn't happen. Hoping that they'd finally get the hint, I rolled my eyes, then started to storm off. "Just leave me alone."

I didn't get far when another biker stepped in front of me, stopping me dead in my tracks. He was just as big and threatening as the other two, but he was older, and there was an unexpected kindness in his eyes—one that made me feel like he was genuinely concerned when he asked, "What's going on here?"

"Nothing," I snapped. "I was just leaving."

Not buying my response, he immediately turned to the other two men, and they were quick to tell him, "We just found her going through the dumpster."

"I already told both of them..." I whipped back around, "I was looking for my keys."

"Oh?" He studied me for a moment, then asked, "And how did they end up there?"

I didn't answer.

I couldn't.

There wasn't an answer to give—at least, not one that made any sense, so I dropped my head and stared at the ground. Seconds later, he asked, "You got a place to go, kid?"

"Why do you care?" These were badass bikers who didn't know me from Adam. I couldn't understand why they were so interested in me and my crappy circumstances. "Why do any of you care?"

"Cause it's thirty degrees out here, and you got no coat," the quiet one clipped. "We're not leaving you out here alone."

"Please just leave it." Tears filled my eyes I told them, "I just gotta make it a couple more months."

"What happens then?"

"I'll be eighteen," I confessed. "I won't have to be put in the system and end up in some place I don't wanna be."

"The way I see it, you got two choices." The older man crossed his arms with determination. "You can either come with us, or we're calling the cops."

"Why would I come with you?"

"We'll get you cleaned up and some real food in your belly." His expression softened as he told me, "And a warm place to lay your head until you get back on your feet. How does that sound?"

"That all sounds great, but what's it gonna cost me?"

"Nothing, kid." I actually believed him when he continued, "Not a damn thing."

Over the last six months, I'd spent countless nights nearly freezing to death in my car. I'd lost so much weight that none of my clothes fit anymore, and I was tired of being so alone. I was tired of always struggling to make ends meet and constantly worrying about where I was going to sleep and how I was going to eat. I was just a kid. I needed help, so I gave him a nod and said, "Okay, I'll come with you."

"That's what I wanted to hear." He motioned his head over to my car as he asked, "You got enough gas to make it across town?"

"Yeah, I got enough." I started towards my car, then quickly stopped and said, "I don't even know your names."

"I'm Cotton." He motioned his head over to his friends as he said, "And Q and Two Bit. You'll meet the others when we get to the clubhouse."

"Are there any women at this clubhouse place?"

"Yeah, there are plenty of 'em."

"Okay. Good to know." He studied me for a moment, then asked, "What about you? Might be helpful to know your real name."

"I'm Elsie Scrogham."

"Scrogham?" Cotton gave me a funny look. "Not exactly a common name around these parts. You any kin to Paul Scrogham?"

"He was my father."

"No kidding." Cotton turned to Q and Two Bit, shook his head, then turned his attention back to me. "I sure hate to hear that he's passed. He was a good fella. Helped us out of tight spot on more than one occasion."

"Can't say I'm surprised. He was awesome like that."

"He most certainly was. I'm glad we've finally got the chance to return the favor."

I gave him a quick nod, then rushed over to my car. By the time I got in and closed the door, they were all on their bikes and waiting. I was hesitant to follow them out of the parking lot, and I even considered ditching them. But then I remembered how lonely and scared I'd felt for the past six months. I wasn't sure that going with these men was the best answer, but it beat spending another night alone in my car.

After a ten-minute drive, we pulled up to a large building that was secured with a tall, metal gate. When I spotted two men standing guard, I felt an overwhelming urge to turn and go the other way, but for reasons I didn't understand, I gathered all the strength I could muster and followed them through that gate. It was the best decision I could've ever made.

I don't know if it was because they all felt indebted to my dad or the fact they were just generous by nature, but two months turned into six years. During that time, the men of Satan's Fury showed me kindness like I'd never known. They gave me a roof over my head, put clothes on my back, and always made sure I had food on my plate. Not only that, but they'd also brought me into their fold and treated me like one of their own. They even gave my parents a proper resting place which I visited often, especially on holidays like today.

It was New Year's Eve. The brothers and their ol' ladies were preparing for a long night of partying, and I was looking forward to joining them. But first, I had some news to share with my parents. I placed a bouquet of flowers on their headstone as I told them, "I made the Dean's list! It was tough, especially with all the stupid papers, but I did it. I actually did it."

I knew they both wanted me to go to college and would be ecstatic with the news. I hated that they weren't there to celebrate with me. While the thought brought tears to my eyes, I quickly brushed them away as I continued, "If all goes well, I'll graduate in a few months, and then, I can get a job and start looking for a place of my own."

A bitter-cold breeze whipped around me and stole my breath. I wrapped my arms around me, clutching my coat as I told them, "I miss you guys. Brantley, too. I can't tell you how much I wish you were here."

My throat tightened, and I was on the verge of tears when I heard a familiar rumble of a motorcycle drawing near. I didn't have to look to see who it was. I already knew it was him. I leaned down and ran my hand across the top of my parents' tombstone as I whispered, "I gotta go... I love you, and I'll be back as soon as I can."

I inhaled a deep breath as I wiped away my tears, then I turned and started back towards the parking lot. When I got to my car, Wyatt was leaning against the passenger door, and the mere sight of him took my breath away. He was tall with a chiseled jaw and athletic physique, and he had this beautiful, dirty blonde hair that was always in such perfect disarray. His penetrating, coal-black eyes seemed to pierce right through me as he asked, "You okay?"

"Um-hmm." I continued over to my side of the car as I told him, "I'm good."

"You sure?"

"Yeah, I'm sure."

From the very start, I'd been crazy about Wyatt. He had this quiet, protective nature that had a way of setting me at ease, and after what I'd been through with my family, I needed that. I needed it more than I realized. It helped ease the brunt of not having my family around, and that meant more to me than he would ever know.

We'd spent countless hours together—sometimes talking while at other times we simply sat together in silence. Any time I was upset or struggling, Wyatt would be there to make sure I got through it. It was one of the many reasons why I loved him.

While I'd never actually said the words, I'd never hidden the way I felt about him. Everyone knew I was crazy about him, but never once had he reciprocated those feelings—at least, not in the way I'd hoped.

Instead, he simply continued acting like we were friends and nothing more. I won't deny it hurt that he didn't return my feelings, and over time, that hurt turned into anger which is why I turned to him with a scowl and spat, "You know, you don't have to keep coming here like this. I'm a big girl. I can handle coming to see my folks on my own."

He didn't respond.

He just stared at me with that deep, soulful look he always had.

I wanted to believe that look meant something, but I'd officially given up hope that he'd ever truly care for me. It was time for me to make a choice. I could keep holding on and hope that he'd finally come around or I could just let go and move on.

Letting go seemed like the most logical answer, but it wouldn't be easy—Wyatt would make sure of that.

CHAPTER 2
Bones

My head was pounding, and I had a terrible case of cotton mouth. I drank too much at the club's New Year's Eve party—which was unusual for me. I rarely touched the stuff. I liked how it made me feel. I liked it a lot. I worried I might end up liking it too much, so I usually did my best to steer clear of the stuff. Drugs, too. But it was New Year's Eve, and the guys were insistent that I stay and party with them.

I agreed, and it wasn't long before I had a beer in my hand. I might've stopped with the one, but then I spotted Elsie tucked away in a corner talking to Hayes. I knew they were just friends but seeing her laughing and bantering with him got under my skin. I had no right to be so bothered. The brothers might've known how I felt about Elsie, but they also knew I hadn't done anything about it.

I hadn't pursued my feelings for her.

I hadn't even tried to claim her.

Simply put—she wasn't mine.

Hayes or any other Joe Blow could stake their claim, and I'd be left out in the fucking cold. And yet, I didn't go over and talk to her at the party. I didn't tell her that she consumed my every thought. Instead, I sat there at the bar with Rooster and Torch and tried to act like I was completely unphased as I drank my weight in booze. It was a decision I would come to regret—not just because of Elsie and Hayes, but because of my massive hangover.

I was struggling.

After I got dressed, I made my way to the kitchen.

When I walked in, several of the guys were sitting at the table eating breakfast, and from the looks of it, they were struggling, too. They were all busy grumbling under their breaths, complaining about their rough morning, so I didn't bother greeting them. Instead, I walked straight over to the medicine cabinet and grabbed a bottle of ibuprofen. I got a couple and tossed them back, praying it wouldn't be long before they started to kick in.

Once I'd returned the bottle, I went over to the

stove, and as I made myself a plate of food, I heard Q say, "Damn, Diesel. You look like hell."

"I feel like hell, too. My head feels like someone is stabbing me in the skull with a dull butter knife, and I'm pretty sure a cat shit in my mouth. Somebody needs to put a fucking bullet in my head." I took my plate over to the table and sat down next to Diesel, listening as he continued, "I can't believe I drank so much last night."

"Hell, it was New Year's Eve." Q chuckled. "We all got a little carried away."

"Carried away is an understatement. I acted a damn fool." Diesel turned a bit green as he asked, "Who was the wise-ass who brought the Mad Dog 20/20?"

"Pretty sure that was Chains."

"Well, he needs his fucking ass kicked." Diesel shook his head as he complained, "I haven't had that nasty shit since I was in my fucking teens, and I couldn't get my hands on anything else."

"You certainly seemed to be enjoying it last night." Q chuckled as he turned to me and said, "Bones did, too."

"Enjoy is not the term I'd use." I grimaced as I remembered the stout taste of soured berries and alcohol. "Not that it mattered. By the time we cracked open the second bottle, I didn't care what the fuck it tasted like."

"Me neither. That's why I'm in the shape I'm in now." Diesel took a long drink of his water, then looked at me and scowled. "How come you don't look like death warmed over?"

"That's just because I'm better looking than you."

"Um-hmm. Whatever you say, boss."

"I still feel like shit." I ran my hand through my disheveled hair. "Don't think I'll be drinking again for a while."

"I second that," Diesel grumbled.

"Are you three done belly aching?" Savage asked as he sat down with a huff. "Cause we got other things to discuss."

"Such as?"

"I don't know. How about why the hell has it been so fucking quiet for the past three weeks?" Savage's brows furrowed with anger as he snarled, "These assholes highjacked our server, kidnapped, and beat the fuck out of Q and Rooster, and then just gave up? That doesn't make any sense."

"No, it doesn't," Cotton agreed.

Like the rest of us, our president had been biting at the bit to figure out who'd been fucking with us. Big and I had been doing what we could to track them down, but sadly, they'd come and gone without a trace, and we were all left wondering when they'd be back—because there was no doubt that they'd be back.

Savage turned to his father as he said, "Is it just me, or do you have a bad feeling that something's coming?"

"It's not just you, son," Cotton answered. "We all took a moment to catch our breaths and bring in the new year, but now, it's time to get our heads back in the game and prepare for what lies ahead."

"That's just it." Savage looked Cotton dead in the eye. "We don't know what lies ahead, and that's something we've never faced before."

"We've faced it before, son. Just not in your time." He placed his hand on Savage's shoulder as he assured him, "We got through it then, and we'll get through it now."

"How we gonna do that when we don't even know who's been fucking with us?"

"We stay vigilant. Keep our eyes and ears open and stay prepared for anything."

As I sat there listening to my brothers talk about the steps we needed to take, I thought about how much my life had changed since I was a kid. There was a time when I wouldn't have been included in such a conversation—not because I wasn't capable of handling such a heavy topic. I was. But the people in my life didn't seem to think so. They were too focused on what was "wrong" with me to ever notice what was right.

My difficulty adjusting to change and sensitivity to loud noises had my doctor and teachers believing that I'd never be able to fit in with my peers, and my inability to conform would make it difficult to form relationships with them.

They weren't wrong.

I did have issues. Hell, I had a lot of them.

I didn't know it. I didn't really care. As far as I was concerned, I was as normal as the next guy, and for all intents and purposes, I had it pretty good.

I was freakishly smart. I could read about something one time and never forget it. And if I was interested in something, I'd spend hours researching everything I could find on it—almost obsessively so. I could also see things in a way that others couldn't—which gave me an unexpected advantage whenever I had a problem to solve.

I was a hell of a gamer. I would play something over and over until I had it down pat and could beat anyone I came up against. It was that push to excel that got me interested in computer hacking. I already had some background knowledge of computer programming and a baseline vocabulary to draw on, so it wasn't all that difficult. I used what I already knew and dove deeper. I spent hours on end learning everything there was on cybersecurity, networking, and scripting, and with Big's help, I became damn good at it.

I also became good at listening to my mother. I know it sounds cheesy, but I trusted her. So, when she told me to watch and listen to the people around me, I watched and listened. Not because I wanted to. I didn't. But I didn't want to be the things my father had called me even more. It was that mindset that had me doing all kinds of things I didn't want to do.

Eventually, I taught myself how to fit in.

I started interacting with others, and by hanging with the brothers, I even got good at it. Hell, a stranger would have no clue that I even had Asperger's. My improvements weren't the norm, but I did the work. I pushed myself to the limit time and time again, and it paid off.

I was no longer an outsider.

I was a Fury brother, and I was treated as such.

After several minutes of back and forth, Cotton turned to me with urgency in his eyes. "I need you and Big to find something... *anything* we can use to find these guys."

"We'll do our best, Prez."

"I'm counting on you, son. We all are."

"Won't let you down, sir."

Without saying anything more, I stood, and after I carried my plate over to the sink, I headed down the hall to the work room. There was a time when Big and I had our own spaces—each with our own specific equipment and software, but over time, we merged the two and created a computer center like none other. When I walked in, I wasn't surprised that Big was already there and busy at work.

I went over to my desk, and as I sat down, I asked, "What are you working on?"

"I'm trying to locate all the security cameras between here and town and from town to the warehouse where they took Q and Rooster." He leaned back in his chair with a huff. "I figured we could cross reference them between the city and the property owners—see if we can find any that don't belong, but just when I think I've got them all, I come across another one."

"Want me to give you a hand?"

"Yeah." He grabbed the map from his desk and spread it across the table behind him, then said, "Here are the ones I've found and identified ownership on. Once we have them all, we can take a drive and see if we can find any others."

"Sounds like a lot of work."

"I know." There was no missing the frustration in his voice as he explained, "There's something here. I feel it in my gut."

"Then, we'll keep at it until we find a connection."

He nodded, and I walked over to my desk and got to work.

I was often distracted or felt off-center whenever I was trying to work alongside someone, but it was different with Big. He was my mentor. He taught me everything he knew and showed me how to use my love of computers to locate information in ways I never imagined.

We'd been at it for several hours when Big turned to me and asked, "Have you gotten to Lexington Street yet?"

"I'm still on Tate." I could tell by his tone that something was up, so I stood and walked over to him. "Why? Did you find something?"

"I'm not sure." He pulled up the surveillance feed from one of the cameras, then pointed to the screen as he said, "This is the view from the camera on Davenport's car lot."

I leaned in and watched as the camera filtered through four specific locations. I could see the small office, the tiny lot with six lackluster cars, and the side alley. I didn't see anything unusual, so I asked, "What am I looking at?"

"The camera on the corner of the old Shell station across the street." Big pointed to the camera as he told me, "Maybe it's just me, but doesn't that camera look relatively new."

"Yeah, it does."

"So, why would someone put up a camera on a place that has been closed for years?"

"Might belong to someone in the area."

"But who?" He motioned his hand towards the map as he said, "It's just this place and the old car lot on the entire block, and you saw for yourself that it's not on the car lot feed."

"And there's nothing else in that area?"

"Just the Grave's farm, and there's no way his tight ass is gonna pay for a security system." After a few clicks of the keyboard, Big brought up another screen. "There's another one just like it on Johnsonville Corner on the backside of the old schoolhouse."

"Seriously?" The schoolhouse had been abandoned for years, and as far as I knew, there wasn't another residence or business for miles—at least, none that were habitable. Thinking there must be some mistake, I leaned in for a closer look. "But why have a camera out there? There's nothing around for miles."

"Exactly."

"Should we check them out?"

"Grab your coat."

I gave him a nod, then rushed to my room. By the time I made it outside, Big was in his truck waiting for me, and if his expression was any indication, he was eager to get going. I jumped inside with him, and seconds later, we were speeding towards the old Shell station.

When we pulled up, there was no one in sight. Even the car lot across the street seemed deserted—or so we thought. We'd just gotten out of the truck and were making our way to the rear of the station when I heard someone shout, "Can I help you boys with something?"

We both stopped and turned to find a man walking in our direction. He was an older guy, well into his late sixties, and he was wearing a suit that looked to be just as old. Big grumbled a curse under his breath, then held up his hand and waved, "Hey there, Charlie. How ya doing?"

"Can't complain." He continued across the street, and as soon as he made his way over to Big, he extended his hand and said, "Good to see ya, Mike."

"How are things at the lot?"

"Been slow, but they always are when it's this damn cold out."

"Yeah, I imagine it could put a real damper on things."

"It definitely does." He motioned his head towards the station as he asked, "So, what brings you two out here?"

"Just checking out the place."

Mr. Davenport's face lit up as he asked, "You

thinking about buying 'cause I bet Dale will give you a real good deal on the place."

"No, I don't think I'm up for making that kind of investment."

"You sure about that? I bet you and those brothers of yours could make a real go of the place."

"Maybe." Big dragged his teeth over his bottom lip, then motioned his hand over to the corner of the building. "Dale got security on the place?"

"Nah." Mr. Davenport shook his head as he snickered, "That'd cost him a pretty penny, and like most folks around here, he's got a pretty tight grip on his wallet."

"If it's not his, then whose is it?"

"I just figured it was one of the city cameras or something. Not even sure the damn thing works."

I could see the red power light blinking on the side of the camera, so I was quick to interject, "It works."

"Well, I got no idea why anyone would be watching this old place. Nothing of value here." The words had barely left his mouth when he immediately started backpedaling. "Not that it couldn't hold value. The right person could turn it into a gold mine."

"Yeah, yeah," Big blew him off. "So, you don't know anything about the camera."

"Can't say that I do."

"Hmm." Big glanced over at me, then said, "See if the serial number is still on it."

"You got it."

I walked over to the camera and quickly discovered that it was too high for me to see anything. I needed something to stand on, so I gathered a couple of old tires that were propped against the building and stacked them on top of one another. Once I had them secure, I climbed on top and eased on my tiptoes, stretching as tall as I could in hopes of spotting the serial number. As soon as I found it, I pulled out my camera and took a quick picture.

On my way back down, I called out to Big, "I got it."

"Good. Let's head over to Johnsonville Corner and see what we can find on the other one." Big gave Mr. Davenport a pat on the arm as he said, "Good to see ya, Charlie. Hope things pick up at the lot soon."

"Wait! You're leaving?" Mr. Davenport gasped. "What about Dale's place? You still interested in buying?"

"Afraid not."

"Oh." Mr. Davenport looked completely baffled as he watched Big and I start towards the truck. We hadn't gotten far when he shouted, "Why do I get the feeling that you were more interested in that camera than you were in buying the place?"

Big didn't answer.

Instead, he got in the truck and closed the door. As soon as I'd gotten in next to him, he started the truck, and we were on our way to the old schoolhouse. I wanted to believe that Big had discovered our first big lead, but my gut told me it was just another long shot. Either way, we were going to keep digging until we found out who we were dealing with.

CHAPTER 3
Elsie

"You and Hayes looked pretty cozy last night." Lacy gave me one of her looks as she said, "If I didn't know better, I'd say he's got a thing for you."

"Hayes and I are just friends. Nothing more."

"Are you sure about that?" Lacy was one of the club's hang arounds, and even though she was several years older than me, she was my closest friend. She had an easy-going, bubbly personality and loved to stir trouble, so I wasn't surprised when she pushed, "'Cause it sure looked like you two were having a good time."

"We were having a good time."

"So, what's the problem?"

"There is no problem." I shrugged. "I'm just not interested in him that way."

Hayes was a great guy, and I enjoyed spending time with him. I enjoyed spending time with all the guys, but I knew what it would mean if I slept with one of them. One would lead to another and another, and it wouldn't be long before they'd stop seeing me as their little sister and more as an easy lay.

While that might have its advantages, I didn't want to be just another hang-around.

Don't get me wrong. Lacy and the other hang arounds were great. They were sweet, beautiful girls, and I enjoyed working with them. We cleaned together, cooked for the guys together, and even did the brothers' laundry together, but at the same time, we lived very different lives. I had my sights set on earning my college degree and having a successful career while they had their sights set on claiming one of the brothers—any of the brothers.

I, on the other hand, was only interested in one, *and only one*.

And it wasn't Hayes.

Lacy pursed her lips as she said, "Well, you're missing out, honey, 'cause that boy can really get the juices flowing *if you know what I mean*."

"I'm sure he can."

"Oh, come on, Lace. Don't waste your breath." Makayla glanced over at me as she dumped more dirty dishes into the sink. "You know she's only got eyes for Bones."

"That's not true!" I dropped the sponge into the sink, then whipped around to face the girls as I said, "He is just a friend."

"A friend *you pine for on a daily basis.*"

"I don't pine for him, Makayla. At least, I don't anymore. I've moved on," I lied.

"Is that so?"

"Um-hmm." I turned back to washing dishes as I told her, "In fact, I have a date Friday night."

"With whom?"

"Ben," I announced proudly. "He's a guy from my Spanish class, and he's so hot. He's tall with dark hair and the bluest eyes I've ever seen. He's really smart and confident, without being overly confident. You would really like him."

"So, when do we get to meet this new hunk of yours?"

I glanced over my shoulder and was about to answer her when I spotted Wyatt standing in the doorway. I had no idea how long he'd been there, but his blank expression suggested that he'd been there long enough to hear what I didn't want him to hear. His eyes never left mine as he started walking in my direction. My throat tightened, and my heart started to race, making it impossible for me to think, much less speak.

Of course, Lacy had no problem flashing her sexiest of smiles and saying, "Hey there, handsome. I haven't seen much of you lately."

"Been busy." He made his way over to the medicine cabinet, grabbed a bottle of ibuprofen, then turned and started back out of the room. "Have a good one."

"Bye, Sugar. You let us know if you need anything."

"Hm-hmm."

Without saying anything more, he marched out of the room and disappeared into the hall. Once she was certain he was gone, Makayla turned to me and asked, "What was that all about?"

"No clue."

I turned my attention back to the dishes in the sink, hoping that she'd get the hint that I didn't want to talk about Wyatt or his bad mood, but no such luck. "Is it just me, or did he seem even more on edge than usual?"

I didn't respond.

There was no point. They'd made it no secret that they'd often found Wyatt's quiet demeanor to be too intense and off-putting. I tried explaining that he was just a guy who didn't speak unless he had something to say, but they didn't get it. They were used to the other brothers and their loud, boisterous personalities and didn't know what to do with the quiet, brooding personality of Wyatt.

I like the quiet.

I usually found it comforting.

At least, I used to find it comforting.

Today was different.

Today, I got the feeling there was a reason behind his silence, and if I didn't know better, I'd say it had something to do with me. But, then again, I had no real reason to think that. He'd had his chance. If he wanted to make a move, then he would've made it, and that was that.

I continued washing the dishes, and just as I'd hoped, it wasn't long before Makayla changed the topic of the conversation. "You know Reagan's birthday is next weekend."

"That's right. I forgot all about it."

"Well, we've gotta do something special. She's going to be twenty-one!"

"That's right!" Excitement filled Lacy's voice as she suggested, "We should go to the city and try out one of those dance clubs everyone's been raving about."

"That's a great idea!"

"How about you, sourpuss?" Lacy bumped me with her hip. "You up for a big night in the city?"

"Yeah, going to the city sounds like fun."

"That's my girl!" Lacy whipped back around to

Makayla. "You know, we should get a couple of hotel rooms. That way, we won't need to designate a DD."

"That's a great idea."

Makayla threw her hands up over her head and started dancing around the kitchen, and it wasn't long before Lacy joined in. They were still twirling around when I finished washing dishes. I grabbed the drying cloth from the counter and tossed it at Lacy. "Those dishes aren't going to dry themselves."

"Yeah, yeah. I'm on it." She stopped dancing and started over to the sink. "Such a sourpuss."

"But you love me anyway."

"You got that right."

I left Lacy and Makayla in the kitchen and headed down the hall to my room. I went over to my desk and got busy studying for my big Spanish test. I hadn't been at it long when I stopped and took a quick look around my room. It looked so different than the day I first arrived at the clubhouse.

Back then, it just had a desk and a small bed in the corner.

Now, the walls were painted gray, the bed had a new comforter and pillows, and I'd hung several pictures I'd brought from home. It was nice—much better than living in my car, and I liked knowing the guys were just down the hall.

They'd really looked out for me.

They made me feel safe. Not only had they given me a roof over my head, but they had given me a home, and not just because of what my father had done for them. They'd taken care of me because they wanted to, and I would be forever grateful. But I was older now and about to graduate college. It wouldn't be long before I had to start really thinking about my future.

It wasn't like I could live at the clubhouse forever. I needed to get a job—a real job, and I needed to find a place of my own. Just thinking about it made my head spin.

Thankfully, I had some time before I had to start planning my future. I had to graduate before I could get a real job, and in order to graduate, I needed to pass my Spanish test. With that thought, I turned my attention back to my studies, and I spent the next few hours focusing on my classes. By the time I was finished, I was both tired and ready for a bite to eat, so I decided to go check the fridge for leftovers.

I was just about to walk into the kitchen when I heard Henley say, "I saw Bones early, and I swear the boy has grown another foot. I can still remember when he was our sweet, little Wyatt with his little game in his hand."

"Oh, I remember it all too well," Wren replied. "He was a precious little thing, but I gotta tell ya.

Raising him wasn't always easy. He had a bit of a stubborn streak."

"What?" Henley scoffed. "No way."

"I know it's hard to believe, especially now. But we had some rough patches." Wren let out a breath before saying, "Mainly because I pushed him to do things he didn't really want to do."

"All kids need a little pushing from time to time."

"That was definitely true for Wyatt. I remember the summer when Michael and I took him to the beach for the first time. He was only five at the time, and we'd just gotten his Asperger's diagnosis. It wasn't the best time to hit the beach, especially when he was going through this phase where he didn't want to touch or be near anything that felt funny on his skin."

"What happened?"

"Girl, the second that baby's feet hit that sand, he lost it. He started screaming and fussing, and I immediately regretted my decision to go to the beach."

"Oh, no. What did you do?"

"I did the only thing I could. I took his little hand and forced him to walk down that beach." My chest tightened when Wren said, "The screaming only got worse, and it didn't help matters that everyone around was staring at me like I was the worst mother on the planet. And to be honest, I felt like the worst mother on the planet."

"Oh, Wren. I can't imagine how hard that must've been."

"Oh, it was, but it had to be done. He had to learn that he could do the hard stuff." I could hear the emotion in her voice as she said, "And in the end, it was totally worth it 'cause when we finally made it to the ocean, and that water touched his little toes, his entire face lit up. He totally forgot about the fit he'd just thrown. And when I saw that smile on his face, I forgot about it, too. The next day was much better. He knew if he could just get to that water, all would be well. We both learned a big lesson that day."

"That story makes me want to cry." Henley's voice was filled with emotion as she said, "You were a good momma, Wren. You still are."

While I enjoyed hearing Wren's story, I felt guilty eavesdropping on them, so I decided to skip dinner and headed back to my room. I crawled into bed and thought about Wyatt on that beach. I could almost picture the smile on his face when he reached the water for the first time. It was a thought that had me smiling as I drifted off to sleep.

The next few days were filled with various chores around the clubhouse and lots of studying. By the time the weekend rolled around, I was ready for a break. Even more so, I was ready for my date with Ben.

Knowing the brothers would never let me live it

down, I chose not to have him come to the clubhouse and made plans to meet at the restaurant instead. I had no clue what to wear, but Lacy was kind enough to help me piece something together. She even helped me with my hair and makeup, and her face lit up when she saw the final product. "You look incredible! Your guy is gonna flip when he sees you in that dress."

"You really think it's okay?" I tugged at the hem. "It's a little short."

"It's not too short. It's perfect."

"What about the necklace?"

"It's good. I like it."

Lacy and I couldn't have been more different. I was tall and curvy. She was short and thin. She was a club girl, and I was not, far from it. But we did have one thing in common—something that made us closer than either of us could've imagined. We'd both suffered from a tragic past—one that left us both with no family. Lacy's mother and little sister were killed in a tragic car accident, and with her father out of the picture, she was left to fend for herself.

I understood her pain, and she understood mine.

That meant something to us both and was one of the many reasons we spent so much time together. Lacy grabbed my purse from my dresser and offered it to me with a bright smile.

"Now, stop worrying and go have yourself a great time with your hot fella."

"Thanks, Lace."

I gave her a quick hug, then rushed down the hall towards the parking lot. I was just about to reach the back door when I heard Q shout, "Whoa! Where are you running off to dressed like that?"

"I've got a date!" I was running late, so I continued out the door as I answered, "I'll be back in a few hours."

"A date with who?"

Before I could answer, the door closed behind me. I continued out to my car and got inside. I started the engine, and as I started to back out, I spotted Wyatt standing next to his bike. His eyes were fixed on me, and his expression wasn't a good one. He stood there watching as I drove through the gate. Even though it seemed odd, I figured Wyatt was just being Wyatt, and I continued out onto the road and headed towards town.

When I pulled up at the restaurant, I was pleased to see that it didn't look very crowded. I parked, then got out and started for the front door. I was about to head inside when I heard, "Elsie! Hold up!"

I turned and found Ben walking towards me. I couldn't help but smile when I saw that he was wearing khakis and a crisp white button down with loafers--which was quite different than the brothers' jeans and leather vests. I gave him a warm smile as I said, "Hey, Ben. I'm sorry I'm running a little late."

"Don't worry about it. As far as I'm concerned, you're right on time." His eyes skirted over me as he said, "You are totally worth the wait... You look incredible."

"Thank you. You look really nice, too."

"Glad you think so." He reached down and took my hand in his, then led me up to the front door. "I hope you're hungry."

"I'm starving."

"Great."

He held the door open for me and waited as I stepped inside. It was a small, family-owned Italian restaurant with worn leather seating and quaint little lanterns glowing at each table, making it feel warm and inviting. It was the perfect place for a first date. The hostess led us to one of the small booths in the back, and once we were seated, she took our drink orders and offered us each a menu. "I'll go get your drinks while you two take a moment to decide what you want to eat."

"Sounds good. Thanks." Ben studied his menu a moment, then asked, "So, whatcha thinking?"

"I'm not sure. The lasagna is really good here, but I think I'm leaning towards the chicken marsala."

"You can't go wrong with either."

"Yeah, I was kind of thinking the same. What about you? What are you having?"

"I'm not sure. I'm still mulling it over." His face was still buried in his menu when he said, "You know, I'm kind of surprised that you came."

"Really? Why's that?"

"I don't know. Just a feeling, I guess." He glanced up at me as he confessed, "I'm really glad you decided to come, though."

"It's still early. You might change your mind about that."

"I highly doubt it." He looked around the room, then said, "You're the most beautiful woman here. No way I couldn't be happy about spending time with you."

"You're very sweet."

"Just being honest."

He gave me a wink, then studied his menu for a moment longer. Once he decided on an entrée, he motioned the waitress over and gave her our order. As soon as she was gone, Ben rested his elbows on the table and leaned towards me. "So, tell me a little about yourself."

"What do you want to know?"

"Anything. I mean, I know you go to school at PC, and you're taking Spanish two. I'm pretty sure I overheard you say you were in the business program."

"I am. I'm hoping to graduate at the end of this semester."

"That's great. Any idea what you will do after you graduate?"

"I'm still trying to figure that out." I took a sip of my soda, then told him, "I'm hoping something will come up between now and then."

"I'm sure you'll figure it out, but if you don't, my uncle runs the real estate office in Oak Harbor. He also has some rental properties that he needs help managing. Maybe he could find something for you."

While I had no interest in real estate, I thought it was sweet of him to offer his uncle's help. "Thanks. I'll keep that in mind."

"You should. He does really well for himself."

The waitress came over and placed our food on the table, and my mouth started to water when I saw the plate full of chicken marsala. "It looks wonderful."

"Wow." Ben glanced over at my plate and then back to his own. "I think I might've made a mistake."

"I'd be more than happy to let you have a taste or two."

"A taste or two? Hmm." He gave me a playful wink as he flirted, "I gotta say, I like the sound of that."

"The marsala, Ben." I gave him a stern look. "And only the marsala."

"Okay, okay. Understood," he chuckled.

We continued on with our small talk as we ate, and it was nice. Ben was not only handsome, but the perfect gentleman. Sadly, I didn't feel the slightest spark as I sat there across from him. It didn't seem fair. He was so open and easy to talk to. He told me all about his sister and the crazy adventures they'd had when they were kids. And even shared a few funny stories about his roommates and frat brothers.

The more he spoke, the more comfortable we both became. I told him about Lacy and the other girls, and then, he asked a question I'd hoped he wouldn't ask. "So, what about your family? Are you guys close?"

"We were." My throat tightened as I told him, "They both died a few months before my eighteenth birthday."

"Oh, damn. I'm sorry, Elsie. I had no idea."

"It's fine. There's no way you could've known, and it was a long time ago."

"Still. That had to be hard." His eyes were filled with sadness as he asked, "Did you have anyone to help you get through it? A brother or a sister?"

"Afraid not." I didn't like the shift in our light-hearted mood, so I decided not to tell him about Brantley. Instead, I told him, "I was lucky enough to meet some wonderful people who helped me get back on my feet."

"That's great. I'm really glad to hear that." A soft smile crossed his face as he said, "Maybe I can meet these wonderful people some time."

"Maybe so." In hopes of getting our night back on track, I leaned back in my chair and cocked my brow. "Enough about me. I want to know more about you... How 'bout you tell me something you wouldn't typically share on a first date."

"Hmmm. That's a tough one." He thought for a moment, then said, "I guess I'd have to go with the fact that I like chick flicks, especially sappy ones where there's a twist in the end, and the guy and girl end up together."

"Awe. He's a romantic."

"What can I say?" He chuckled with a shrug. "I like a happy ending."

I liked happy endings, too, but I didn't see one in our future—at least, not like the one you'd find in movies. It would take a lot more than a surprise twist for me to land the man of my dreams—it would take a miracle, and unfortunately, miracles were in short supply in stories like mine.

CHAPTER 4
Bones

I hadn't slept a wink.

I'd spent the entire night fixating over Elsie's fucking date. I wanted to know if she'd had a good time with him, if she'd laughed with him, or if she'd told him the stories she'd once told me. I wanted to know if he'd fucking touched her, kissed her, or made plans to see her again. The rational side of me knew it was not my concern. Elsie had every right to go out with whomever she wanted. But my irrational side believed Elsie was mine, and it had me tied up in knots and unable to sleep.

I was tired of tossing and turning, so I decided to just give it up. I got out of bed and headed to the bathroom. After I turned on the shower, I took off my clothes, then stepped under the hot stream of water. In a matter of seconds, I could feel the tension in my body start to dissipate, but sadly, it did little to distract me from how incredible Elsie looked when she left for her date. Every time I closed my eyes, I saw Elsie staring at me with one of her heated looks, and it only made my cock ache even more.

When I couldn't take it any longer, I reached down and wrapped my fingers around my thick cock, then slowly started stroking up and down. My breath quickened as I imagined Elsie in my arms. Her body close. Her breasts pressed against my chest. One thought led to another, and it wasn't long before I was imagining her in my bed with her little whimpers and moans echoing through the room.

Everything about her had me spiraling more and more out of control. Her smile. Her voice. Her scent. Fuck. That's all it took. My breath caught, and I came long and hard. I hoped it would be enough to take the edge off and to ease the tension that was building in my gut, but as I stepped out of the shower and started drying off, I quickly realized the knot in my stomach was still there.

I knew then it was going to be a long day.

I threw on my clothes, brushed my teeth, and headed to the conference room to meet up with Big. We were meeting with Cotton and the others to discuss the intel we'd gathered, but there was just one problem.

The intel was useless.

All of it.

"We're wasting our time. We've been through all this." Big tossed one of the files across the table as he huffed, "If there was something to find, we would've already found it."

"I thought you guys found something with the cameras."

"It was another dead end." Big motioned his hand over the stack of intel we'd collected over the past few weeks and groaned, "It's all just a bunch of dead ends."

"He's right." Big and I spent days going from one camera to the next, but each and every one of them ended up being a waste of our fucking time. They were either no longer in service or belonged to someone in the area. I lowered my head in shame as I pushed my chair away from the table. "We've been over and over this shit, and there's nothing to be found."

"I think it's time we changed our perspective on things." Maverick stood and started pacing back and forth as he said, "Instead of focusing on what we don't know, let's focus on what we do."

"Not sure I'm following," Big answered.

"What do we know about these guys?"

"We don't know shit," Q grumbled.

"That's not true." Maverick stopped pacing as he

said, "We know they hacked into our server, and not just anybody could do that shit."

"Yeah, and even after we shut them down, they were still able to keep eyes on us." Big leaned back in his chair as he added, "They had to be watching Q and Rooster. There's no other way they could've gotten to them so easily."

"*Hey... Ho*. There wasn't anything easy about it," Rooster argued. "We made them work for that shit."

"Oh really?" Maverick cocked his brow as he teased, "'Cause from what I saw, it looked like they ran you off that fucking road like a couple of girls on a blind date."

"Whatever, brother. Last time you got rammed was in your bedroom, and I doubt you took it any better than we did."

"Focus, boys. Focus," Cotton fussed.

Rooster and Maverick exchanged a couple of disgruntled looks, but both knew better than to say anything. The room fell silent until Stitch finally mentioned, "They had access to one of the portside warehouses."

Big ran his hand over his beard as he added, "And they had to have eyes on it, too. Probably on both the entryway and the actual warehouse. It's the only way they knew we were coming."

"But how are they pulling it off?" I ran my hand

over my face with frustration. "I mean, I get having security cameras on site, but on the road? It doesn't make sense."

"Unless they're cops," Two Bit grumbled under his breath.

"I doubt Harris or Daniels have anything to do with this." Cotton shook his head as he grumbled, "Hell, those two can barely tie their fucking shoes."

"Well, they can tail with the best of 'em," Clutch complained. "Harris followed me for almost an hour. From work to the gas station, and then on to the house. It was weird."

"Now that you mention it, he followed me around for a while last week," Rooster confessed.

"Daniels tailed me for a while the other night. He was parked outside the construction site and followed me home. Did the same last night." Guardrail turned to Cotton as he said, "It's doubtful that they have anything to do with this, but you gotta admit, the timing is awfully suspicious."

"Yeah, it might be time for us to have a conversation with our men in blue."

"I think you might be right." Cotton turned to Stitch as he said, "You and Wrath go have a chat with Daniels and see if you can get anything out of him."

"You got it."

I wasn't surprised that Cotton wanted them to

start with Daniels. He and Cotton had history that dated back long before my time. His son had run into some trouble, and Cotton called in a favor and made it disappear. Since then, the two had been allies of sorts. If there was something to tell, I had no doubt that Daniels would tell it.

Stitch and Wrath stood and walked out of the room, and Two Bit was the first to ask, "And what about us? Anything you need us to do?"

"Stay on high alert." His tone softened as he added, "I know it's quiet. I know it might seem like these guys have given up and moved on, but I think we all know that's not the case."

"Yeah, we don't have luck like that," Maverick scoffed. "These guys are out there, and it's only a matter of time before they rear their ugly heads. But you don't gotta worry, Prez. We'll be ready when they do."

"That's what I wanted to hear." With that, Cotton turned to Big and me. "You two have been at this for weeks. It's time for you to take a break and step away from this shit for a bit."

"Nah, we're good, Prez," Big argued. "We don't need a break."

"It's not up for discussion." Cotton's eyes narrowed. "You're done for the day. You can start fresh tomorrow."

Big gave him a nod. "Whatever you say, boss."

"Church is dismissed."

Cotton stood, then immediately followed Guardrail and Maverick out of the conference room. I sat there for a moment, trying to steady the mix of guilt, shame, and all-consuming anger that was brewing in the pit of my stomach. Even though I knew Big and I had done everything we could possibly do, I couldn't help but feel like I'd let the brothers down, and that didn't sit well with me. In fact, it had me all kinds of fucked up.

Sensing my distress, Stitch came over and placed his hand on my shoulder. "This isn't over, son. We'll find 'em."

"I know." I glanced up at him as I said, "I just hate we haven't been able to track them down."

"Tomorrow's a new day." He gave me a fatherly pat, then said, "Go get away for a bit. Blow off some steam and clear your head. It'll do you good."

I nodded, then stood and walked out of the room. Without saying a word to anyone, I continued down the hall and out to the parking lot. I was on edge and in dire need of some lengthy wind therapy, but as luck would have it, it was too fucking cold for the Harley. Having no other choice, I got in my truck and drove through the clubhouse gate. As soon as I was on the open road, I hammered down on the accelerator and sped down the old, winding road that led to my house.

My head was all over the place.

One minute I was thinking about the guys and what was going on with the club, and then, I was thinking about Elsie and how incredible she looked when she left for her fucking date. It was just another twist of the knife. I hated that I'd let things with her get to this point. I had no one to blame but myself.

At first, I didn't think anything of the draw I felt towards her.

I thought it was just a really strong friendship. It wasn't until the night of Savage's birthday party that I realized our connection was something more.

Savage had just patched in, and the brothers were hell-bent on showing him the night of his life. They'd packed the place with friends, ol' ladies, and hang arounds. Some were playing beer pong, while others were busy shooting darts or playing pool. All were drinking heavily, and while it looked like a great time, I wasn't in the mood to get wasted.

It had been a long, fucking week, and I just wanted to sit by the fire and clear my head. Unfortunately, that wasn't going to happen. I was on my way out the back door when Rooster shouted, "Yo, Bones. Get over here and play a round with us."

"Sorry, man. I'm heading out."

"Come on, brother." Rooster nodded over to the beer pong table as he complained, *"These girls are kicking my ass! I'm pretty sure they're cheatin'."*

"We're not cheating." Elsie giggled as she told him, *"You just suck."*

"And they're mean, too!" Rooster shook his head. *"Damn. I need your steady hand to help me turn things around."*

"Fine, but only one round."

"One round is all I need."

I walked over to the table and stood beside Rooster. There were only a couple of solo cups left on his side but a full triangle at the other end. Rooster wasn't exaggerating when he said the girls were kicking his ass. "Damn, Roost. You really do suck."

"I don't suck. I'm just a little off tonight." He nodded towards Lacy as he whispered, *"Lace and that short skirt of hers are fuckin' with my head. If I lose, I'm gonna look like a schmuck. You gotta help me out."*

He placed a ping pong ball in my hand, then stepped to the side, holding his breath as I dipped the ball in the water and tossed it across the table. When it landed in the center of one of the cups, Rooster slammed his fist into my bicep and shouted, "Hell, yeah!"

"Well, done," Lacy smirked at Rooster. *"Now, let's see if you can actually make one this time."*

A look of determination crossed his face as he stepped

over, dipped the ball, and tossed it across the table. Like many times before, the ball missed the cups by a mile. He dropped his head and cursed, "Dammit."

"Our turn!" Elsie stepped and took her shot, and the ball sank into the cup. "Yes!"

"If I get this last one, we win." Lacy got into position and took her shot, and when it dropped inside the cup, she jumped up and down. "And that's how it's done."

"I demand a rematch!" Rooster fussed.

"I'd be down for that." Elsie smiled at me as she asked, "What about you? You want to play another round?"

"Yeah, I could do one more round." Knowing Rooster was itching to hook up with Lace, I suggested, "Why don't we make it interesting and swap partners?"

"I'd be good with that."

"Me, too." Lacy sauntered over to Rooster and bumped him with her hip. "What do you think, partner?"

"I think we're kicking some ass."

"Don't you know it!" She lifted her hand, giving him a quick high five, and then she turned to Elsie. "You two ready?"

"Absolutely." Elsie gave me a wink as she said, "Let's show 'em how it's done."

Unlike the other girls, Elsie wasn't overly done up. She was wearing a vintage Van Halen t-shirt she'd gotten from her favorite thrift shop and a pair of baggy jeans, and her long, red hair was pulled up in a messy bun. Her relaxed look mirrored her easygoing personality. It was part of her charm, and one of the many reasons I enjoyed hanging out with her.

Elsie and I set up the cups, and after just a few shots, we had a pretty good lead. And I have to admit, I was having a pretty good time. I took another shot, and as soon as I made it, Elsie started dancing around in the crowd. "We're on fire."

Our game had gathered a few onlookers, including Savage, who slurred, "Yes, you are," as he sauntered over. "Damn, girl. You're looking all kind of good tonight."

"Thanks, but I think you might have your beer googles on."

"No, I'm good." A smirk crossed his face as he said, "I'd be even better if you came over here and planted those sexy lips on mine."

"I'm good right where I am. Thanks."

"You'd be even better over here with me."

A knot was growing in the pit of my stomach, and with every word out of Savage's mouth, it was growing bigger and bigger. I didn't like the way he was speaking to her and looking at her, and I had to fight the urge to knock him flat.

Savage was the president's son and one of my closest friends. The last thing I wanted to do was get into a round with him, but seeing him disrespect Elsie had me seeing red.

He took another slug off his beer, then staggered closer to Elsie. He dropped his arm over her shoulder, then drew her into his chest. "Why don't you and I continue the party back in my room?"

"I don't think so, Ace."

"Why not? I'd show you a real good time."

"I'm sure you would, but I'm not interested."

She gave him a bit of a shove, pushing him off her. He stumbled a bit, then complained, "Come on, baby. Don't be like that."

"I think you got your sights set on the wrong girl, brother," I said to Savage.

He looked at me, then back over at Elsie. He studied her for a moment, then to my pleasant surprise, he shrugged and walked away. Knowing he was drunk, Elsie didn't think much of their little exchange and continued on with the game. I, on the other, couldn't stop thinking about it.

I knew then that what I felt for Elsie was more than friendship.

I tried to fight it, but over the years, that feeling only grew stronger.

Needless to say, I wasn't happy about her going out with some other guy, but sadly, there wasn't a damn thing I could do about it.

The drive to the house had not improved my mood. In fact, it had only made it worse, and it didn't help matters that it was dark, and my place looked abandoned. I wasn't exactly surprised. I hadn't been home in over a week, and even then, I'd just come by to grab some clean clothes. I headed inside and dropped my keys on the counter. I stood there for a moment, just looking around at the place I called home.

The three-bedroom condo was relatively modern, with sleek lines and a muted color palate. The mix of dark grays and blacks gave it a masculine feel without making it feel too cold and uninviting. It could use a good cleaning, but I wasn't in the mood. I was on edge and feeling restless, like a clock that had been wound too tight, and I was struggling to pull myself together.

Part of it was just your typical pent-up frustration, but there were times, like now, when I had a difficult time dispelling the feeling. I tried distracting myself by watching some television and fiddling with my phone, but the unease and disquiet remained in the background. I needed something more, so I turned off the TV, got up from the sofa, and headed to my room to change clothes. I put on a black button-down with a pair of black slacks and black shoes, then grabbed my keys and headed out to my truck, leaving my Fury cut behind.

An hour later, I was in the city, parked at one of

the most popular nightclubs around. There was a time when I'd avoid a place like this at all costs. The loud music and flashing lights would send me straight into sensory overload, and I would shut down. I hated that something so trivial had such an effect on me. It made me feel powerless and weak.

I refused to let anything have that kind of control over me, so I forced myself to listen to the music, face the strobe lights, and mingle with the large crowds. At first, it was brutal. I could only take a few minutes at a time, but with each attempt, I was able to withstand it a little longer and a little longer. Some might call it torture, and in some regards, it was.

I couldn't process it. I would experience extreme agitation like my nerves were being ground down with sandpaper, and it wouldn't be long before the panic would set in.

My entire body would tense.

My pulse would quicken.

My palms would sweat.

My head would pound.

It would take every ounce of determination I could muster to fight the urge to lash out and cause someone else the kind of anguish I was feeling.

But I didn't give in to those urges.

Instead, I stayed and faced my demons.

I let them push me to the brink, time and time

again, and the second I fell off that cliff—when I finally broke, it was like exhaling a breath I didn't know I was holding. All the anxiety and panic would fade, and I was finally able to reset.

I needed that reset tonight. It was the only thing that could distract me from the growing knot in my stomach. I knew I could find it here.

I inhaled a deep breath, then got out of the truck and headed inside. As soon as I opened the front door, I was hit with blaring music and flickering lights. I pressed forward, and it wasn't long before I could feel my senses getting heightened. I made my way over to the bar and sat down. One of the female bartenders came over. She was attractive, petite, with long blonde hair and fake eyelashes.

She leaned forward, revealing a hint of cleavage as she said, "Hey there, handsome. What can I get ya?"

"I'll take a club soda."

"You sure I can't get you something a little stronger? We've got Blue Moon on tap tonight."

"The club soda will be fine. Thanks."

"Sure thing." She gave me a wink, then turned to get my drink. Moments later, she returned, placing the glass down on a napkin as she purred, "Let me know if you need anything else."

I gave her a quick nod, then turned to face the dance floor.

A popular song came on, and the crowd went wild. Young and old, gay and straight, black and white, all rushed for the dancefloor. I, on the other hand, stayed put. I never danced. I simply sat back and soaked in my surroundings. There are so many people, all dancing like they don't have a care in the world. The flashing strobe lights made each of their movements seem like they'd paused between blinks.

I just sat there, fixated on the mirage of bodies, and I finally was starting to decompress when I saw her. She was dancing with Lacy and several other club hang arounds, and I'd never seen her look quite so beautiful. She was wearing a little black dress that hugged her curves in all the right places, and her fiery-red hair cascaded down her delicate shoulders.

I'd always liked watching Elsie, and tonight was no different. The music seemed to move through her like she was a puppet on a string. She looked so free, so alive, as she swayed her hips to the rhythm of the music, and I couldn't remember the last time I'd seen her smile the way she was tonight. It felt good to see her look so happy. I could've sat there watching her for hours.

But then, everything went to shit.

She was dancing with the girls, minding her own business, when a guy came up behind her. He reminded me of Taylor Kitsch with his beach-bum hair and surfer build. He didn't come off as a threat until he slipped his arm around her waist and pulled her back against his chest. At first, she just smiled and went with it, dancing to the rhythm he set for them, but then, he pulled her a little closer—too close. Shaking her head, she gave his hand a shove and took a step away from him.

Noting Elsie's struggle, Lacy stepped up next to her, trying to block the guy from getting close again, but he didn't take the hint. He came back over to her, snaked his hand back down around her waist, then pulled her back against his chest. She tried to break free from his hold, but he was too strong.

This wasn't like the night Savage overstepped.

This guy was a stranger in a crowded bar. There wasn't a clubhouse full of bikers there to protect her and make sure the asshole didn't go too far. And to make matters worse, she looked like she'd been drinking. Elsie gave him another shove, and rage surged through me when I saw her say, "Let me go."

The guy refused, and I was done.

I lunged from my seat and charged towards them.

I kept my eyes trained on Elsie as I plowed through the crowd. When I reached them, I said nothing. I gave no warning. I simply reared back my fist and plowed it into the guy's jaw. He released his hold on Elsie as he stumbled back and grumbled, "What the fuck!"

"Wyatt!" Elsie gasped. "What are you doing here?"

The asshole who had a hold on Elsie pushed her to the side, then rammed his chest into mine. "What's your fucking problem, dickhead?"

"She told you to let go! You should've listened!"

He studied me for a moment, then looked to his buddy as he scoffed, "Is this guy for real?"

"Let's bolt, man. These chicks ain't worth it."

"Fuck no." His words were riddled with anger as he said, "This motherfucker isn't running me off."

He reached for Elsie once again, tugging her over to his side, and I saw red. "Take your fucking hands off her."

I grabbed him by the collar, then reared back and punched him. Then I punched him again and again. I would've hit him once more if Elsie hadn't tugged at my arm and urged, "Wyatt! Stop!"

I released his collar, and he immediately fell back, landing on the floor with a thud. No one around seemed to care about the brawl. Instead, they just kept dancing and having a big time. Elsie, on the other hand, looked positively livid. "What the hell are you doing?"

She perched her hands on her hips as she snapped, "You know, I could've handled him. I didn't need you going all Conan on him!"

I couldn't exactly tell her the truth—that I was

crazy about her and hated seeing that asshole's hands on her, so I tried to think of another plausible excuse. None came to mind, so I simply stood there and stared back at her, which only seemed to make her madder. "I don't get it. What are you even doing here?"

Again, I had no reasonable response, so I turned and started out of the club. Elsie immediately called out, "Wait! Where are you going?"

I continued walking and was just about to reach the door when I heard Elsie shout, "Wyatt! Stop!"

I turned and found her rushing towards me with a flustered look on her face. As soon as she made her way over to me, she asked, "What are you doing? What was all that?"

"You need to be more careful."

"Why do you even care?"

"*You know why.*"

Without saying anything more, I turned and walked out the door.

CHAPTER 5

Elsie

I can still remember the day I fell in love with Wyatt.

I'd been living at the club for a couple of months, and things were going pretty well. I was finally starting to adjust to being at the clubhouse. It wasn't exactly hard. The brothers had been unbelievably sweet to me. They were very attentive and kind, and they made sure I had everything I could possibly need and more. For the most part, things were good, but I still had bad days.

I still missed my old life.

I still missed my family.

And on this particular day, I was missing them terribly.

I thought some fresh air might help me shake my blues, so I went outside and sat down at one of the picnic tables. I tried to focus on the trees and the sounds of the birds singing, but my mind continued to drift to my parents. I couldn't stop thinking about my mother's scent, my dad's goofy laugh, and my brother's sweet smile.

They were the light of my life, and the thought that they were no longer in my life brought tears to my eyes. As soon as one tear fell, the dam broke, and I started sobbing.

I had no idea how long I'd been crying when I felt someone sit down next to me. They didn't say a word. They didn't have to. I knew it was Wyatt. He was the only man I knew who would come there to check on me. When my tears finally ran dry, I wiped my eyes and muttered, "It's been a rough morning."

"Any particular reason why?"

"No." I shrugged. "Just missing my folks."

"I'd say that's reason enough." Wyatt lowered his head. "I can't imagine what this has been like for you."

"I can't get that night out of my head." I could feel my tears building as I told him, "When I walked in, I thought they'd just fallen asleep. It was awful, Wyatt. Just awful. I don't want to remember them that way."

"Then don't. Focus on the good memories, and it won't be long before they're the only ones you will remember."

"But the good ones are harder to remember."

"Maybe, but they're there. You just gotta give it

time." Wyatt leaned back as he said, "Why don't you tell me one of your favorite memories of your mother?"

"Okay, that's an easy one." I smiled as I told him, "Whenever I was sick, she would spend the entire day looking after me. We would lay in bed and watch movies for hours, and when I got hungry, she'd make me some chicken noodle soup and one of her famous grilled cheese sandwiches."

"Sounds like she was a pretty awesome mom."

"She definitely was."

"Hate I missed out on her famous grilled cheese. They're one of my favorites."

"I know her secret. I'll make you one sometime."

"I'd like that."

And just like that, my bad day wasn't so bad.

The next day, I came home from class and found a small journal on my bed. I picked it up, and tears filled my eyes when I read the note that was taped on the front.

For the good memories.

It was a simple gesture, but it changed things between Wyatt and me. I no longer saw him as just another brother. He was now the man who had stolen my heart, and everyone knew it. I'd tried, but I couldn't seem to hide how I felt about him—especially from Lacy and the girls.

They were very invested in our story, so I wasn't exactly surprised when Makayla announced, "I still can't believe Bones was at the club last night."

"Yeah, I didn't even know he went to places like that." We were in the laundry room, working on the club's laundry—one of the many tasks Lacy and the others helped with, and it didn't take us long to start talking about the wild night we'd had. Lacy's eyes narrowed as she asked, "Why do you think he was there... You think he followed us there?"

"Why would he do that?"

"So he could keep an eye on you?" Lacy pulled the rest of the clothes from the dryer and placed them in the hamper. "It's not like he hasn't done it before."

"Yeah, but this is different. This time he punched a guy."

"All the more reason for you to talk to him."

"I've tried, but I can't seem to catch him alone. He's always busy with the guys." I walked over and started helping her fold as I told her, "Not that it matters. I doubt he would talk to me about it."

"Probably not."

Makayla rolled her eyes. "Men can be so hard-headed sometimes."

"Yeah, they most definitely can."

I'd gone over the events of last night a hundred times, and I simply couldn't understand how everything had gotten so messed up. I was having such a great time with Lacy and the girls—even better than I thought I would. We'd been talking about going all week, and the nightclub we went to was everything they promised it would be and more. The energy of the crowd was positively electric, and it didn't take long for that energy to rub off on all of us. Reagan ordered us a round of shots, and we'd barely gotten them down before she ordered another.

We were considering having another when one of our favorite songs came on, and we all bolted for the dance floor. We formed our own little circle and started dancing to the beat of the music. It wasn't long before two guys came over to join us. They were both relatively handsome and seemed like okay guys, but I didn't think much about it. I wasn't usually one to draw the attention of men like them, especially when I was with the girls.

I continued dancing, and to my surprise, one of the men stepped up behind me and started dancing. At first, I was flattered and just went with it. Then, everything went south.

I shook my head as I muttered, "He really did a number on that guy."

"Yes, he did."

"Well, we all know how passionate Bones can be."

"What's that supposed to mean?"

Lacy gave Makayla a stern look, and she quickly lowered her head. "Nothing."

"No, there's definitely something."

"It's nothing. Really."

I wanted to believe her, but I could tell by the way she and Lacy were exchanging looks that she wasn't being completely forthright. At first, I couldn't figure out what they were keeping from me, and then, it hit me like a ton of bricks. "Hold on... Did you two hook up?"

"Well..." Again, she glanced over at Lacy, then finally admitted, "Just a couple of times. We didn't think anything of it."

"We?" I Immediately turned to Lacy. "You hooked up with him, too?"

"It was a long time ago, Else."

I felt both heartbroken and embarrassed. All the single guys hooked up with them, and it only made sense that Wyatt would, too. I just didn't want to think about Wyatt being with anyone else, especially not one of my best friends. My throat tightened as I gasped, "How could you not tell me?"

"Because it wasn't a big deal." Worry marked her face. "You know how it is with the guys and us. We all hope they will someday fall for us and claim us as their ol' lady, but that never happens."

"And we all know how you feel about Bones," Makayla added. "Telling you about it would just be making something outta nothing. And like Lacy said, it was a long time ago."

"How long ago?"

"A couple of months after you moved in," Lacy answered. "Just before you and I started getting close. I'm sorry. I know I should've mentioned it to you, but I didn't want you to hate me."

"I could never hate you, Lace." I let out a breath, then said, "I just wish you would've told me."

"Yeah, me too. I'm sorry I didn't." Lacy came over and gave me a quick hug. "Forgive me?"

"Yeah, I forgive you."

After a brief embrace, we both turned back to folding laundry. It didn't take long for my mind to drift to a place it had no business drifting, and before I realized what I was doing, I asked, "So, what exactly did you mean by passionate?"

"Hmmm?"

"Wyatt."

"Oh." Makayla wouldn't look at me as she explained, "He was just a little intense at times."

I didn't have a lot of experience with sex. In fact, I didn't have any.

I'd never been with a man. I hadn't actually planned to remain a virgin. I wasn't sitting high on some moral ground. I was simply focused on surviving, getting through school, and keeping my head above water. Crawling in bed with a man wasn't a priority. Besides, the only guy I was truly interested in being with wasn't exactly interested in being with me—at least, not the way I wanted him to be.

But I did live at the Satan's Fury clubhouse. I had seen and heard things that would make the devil himself blush. On top of that, I had quite an imagination—and that imagination was running wild. One second, I was imagining him as a straight missionary type of guy with an occasional slap of the ass or pull of the hair, and then the next, he was full-on Dom, giving seductive orders to his submissive. Both of which were intriguing and terrifying at the same time.

I should've left it, but I just kept pushing. "Intense?"

"Don't."

"Don't what?"

"Don't ask questions you don't want the answer to."

"Yeah, she's right. Just leave it," Makayla piped in. "Besides, you'll find out soon enough."

"Um, nooo..." I rolled my eyes. "He's not into me that way."

"You're crazy. The man is totally into you." Lacy smirked at Makayla. "He proved that last night."

"*He was just being protective.*"

"It was much more than that." Makayla sounded very sure of herself as she added, "The guy's got a soft spot for you. He just needed a little push to see it, and if you ask me, I'd say he needs another one."

"What kind of push?"

"I don't know." I could see the wheels turning in her head, and when she smiled mischievously, I knew I was in trouble. "What about that guy you went out with the other night?"

"He was okay and all, but I just wasn't interested. I kind of felt like I was having dinner with my cousin or something."

"Well, Bones doesn't have to know that." Her smirk widened as she suggested, "For all he knows, you two really hit it off and are planning your next date."

"She's right!" Lacy looked like she was about to burst with excitement when she suggested, "You should set up another date with him and tell him to come here to pick you up."

Just thinking about how the guys would react to me having a guy come to the clubhouse made me groan, "You know the guys would never let me live that down."

"Oh, don't worry about them." Lacy lifted her

hand, waving it nonchalantly. "They'll be fine. And even if they do give you a little hell about it, it'll be worth it to see how Bones reacts."

"You really think so?"

"Absolutely."

"Okay... I guess it's worth a shot."

I pulled out my phone and sent Ben a message, asking him if he'd like to hang out again. I didn't even have time to put my phone back in my pocket before he replied, saying that he would love to get together. A few texts later, we had made plans to go out to eat and watch a movie. I'd even done like the girls had suggested and asked him to pick me up.

I felt a little guilty about not telling him that the address I'd given him was to the Fury clubhouse, but I didn't want to take a chance on him not showing. I figured he'd only be there for a few minutes, so I thought it wouldn't be a big deal.

I was wrong.

I'd picked out the perfect outfit—a classic miniskirt with a long, cable-knit sweater and knee-high boots, I'd curled my hair, and I'd gone all out with my makeup. I was looking pretty good. It seemed a shame to waste it on a guy I wasn't all that interested in, but I held on to the hope that Lacy and Makayla were right about Bones and this little charade would pay off.

Lacy was all smiles as she said, "You look great."

"You really think so?"

"Oh, yeah. Bones isn't going to know what hit him."

"I don't even know if he's here."

"Oh, he is. I just saw him walking down the hall with Big and Rooster."

My phone chimed with a message, and my throat tightened when I saw that it was from Ben. He was letting me know that he was about to pull in, and that thought had my heart racing. "Are you sure about this?"

"Nope."

"Lace!"

"I'm kidding! It's going to be fine. Besides, it's too late to back out now."

The words had barely left her mouth when there was a pounding at my door. "Hey, Elsie!"

"Yeah?"

"There's a dude at the gate. Chains said he was here to see you."

"Great! I'm coming."

I opened my door and found Wyatt and Rooster standing in the hall. Wyatt's mouth dropped the second he saw me. I could feel the heat of his eyes as they skirted down my body, sending chills down my spine. Damn. I loved when he looked at me like that. For a moment, I thought he was going to say something, but he simply stood there, glaring at me like a hungry predator.

Rooster's expression was fierce as he asked, "So, you were expecting this guy?"

"Of course, I was." I inhaled a quick breath, then slipped past them. "He's my date."

"Your date?" Rooster followed as I headed towards the back door. "And you didn't think to mention that he was coming here?"

"*I did mention it*... I told Cotton about it this morning."

"You did?"

"Of course, I did." I stopped and turned to face them. "I wouldn't bring someone here without telling him."

Rooster crossed his arms and gave me a scowl. "So, who is this guy?"

"Nobody." I shrugged. "He's in one of my classes. He's perfectly innocent."

"No one is innocent, Elsie. No one."

Our exchange drew the attention of Savage and Torch. They'd both come out of their rooms and made their way over to us. Savage looked and sounded just like Cotton as he turned to Rooster and asked, "What the hell is going on?"

"Elsie invited some guy over here."

"Did you run it by Cotton?"

"*Yes*," I groaned with frustration. "I ran it by Cotton."

Our little plan was going south, and it was going south fast. Things only got worse when the back door opened, and Chains stepped in with Ben. Even though he was just as tall and muscular, his khakis and a neatly pressed button-down made Ben look small and weak next to the guys. Chains looked positively livid when he announced, "He says he's here to see Elsie."

"Elsie?" Ben looked understandably rattled when he turned to me and asked, "What is this place? Who are these guys?"

"We're Satan's fucking Fury, asshole." Rooster stepped towards him, stopping just inches from his face. "Who the fuck are you?"

"Ben Nichols. I'm... ah." He stepped back, only stopping when he bumped into the back door. "Like I told the other guy, I'm just here to pick up Elsie. I don't want any trouble."

Even though he was behind me and I couldn't get a good look at him, I could feel Wyatt's eyes on me. They were burning against my flesh as I reached for Rooster's arm and said, "Please, stop. You're making too much of this. We're just going to the movies."

"I think it's best if I just go."

Ben gave the back door a push, then slipped outside. I gave Rooster and Chains a harsh look, then rushed past them and out the door. Ben was just about to get in his car when I finally caught up to him. "Ben! Please wait!"

"What the hell was that?"

"That was the guys being overly protective." I knew it was much more than that, but I didn't know how else to explain it. "I'm really sorry."

His expression softened as he said, "It's not your fault."

"It kind of is." I glanced behind me and sighed when I saw that Rooster and Wyatt were standing at the back door watching us. "I should've told them you were coming."

"You could've told me, too. It would've been nice to know that I was coming to the Satan's Fury clubhouse. I could've been a little more prepared."

"Yeah, that was bad, and again, I'm really sorry."

"It's fine. Don't worry about it." He paused for a moment, then asked, "Do you still want to go grab a bite?"

"I'd like that."

"Great."

He walked over and opened the passenger side door, then waited for me to get inside. Once I was settled, he closed the door, then got in next to me. As soon as we were both buckled in, Ben started the car, and we were on our way. We hadn't been riding long when he turned to me and asked, "How the hell did a girl like you end up living at the Satan's Fury clubhouse?"

"Remember me telling you that some friends helped me out when my parents died?" He nodded. "Well, they are the friends. I had no place to go, and they took me in."

"Your parents died just before you turned eighteen, right?"

"Yes, that's right."

"So, you've been living there for six years?"

"I have." I could tell by his tone that he was struggling with the idea, so I added, "I know they didn't make a very good impression, but I promise, they're really good guys. They gave me a place to stay and looked out for me."

"You didn't have any family or friends who could've taken you in?"

"No, I had no one. I honestly don't know what I would've done without them."

"I see."

Our conversation trailed off when we pulled up to the pizzeria. But as soon as we were inside and seated, Ben started in with more and more questions—some of which I wasn't sure how to answer. "So, they just took you in."

"Pretty much."

"Hmm." He seemed perplexed by the thought, so I wasn't surprised when he asked, "How well do you know them?"

"Well enough, I guess."

"Okay, then, what's their story?" He took a sip of his beer, then asked, "What are they into?"

"I'm not sure what you mean."

"Is it just drugs, or are they running guns, too?"

"What makes you think..."

"Oh, come on, Elsie. Don't act like you don't know," he scoffed. "You live under the same roof. You gotta know they aren't just riding bikes. These guys are into some pretty heavy shit."

"You don't know what you're talking about."

"Seriously? You're gonna tell me you haven't heard the rumors about them?"

"I have." I leaned back in my chair as I added, "But rumors are just rumors. Nothing more."

"But they're not just rumors." I didn't like his condescending tone. And I really didn't like when he said, "They're facts."

"You know, I think it might be best that we end things here."

"What?" His brows furrowed. "What are you talking about?"

"This date is over." I stood and placed a twenty on

the table, paying for my part of the meal. "I'll find my own way home."

"You gotta be kidding me!" When I turned and started for the door, he shouted, "Elsie, wait! I'm sorry!"

His apology came too little too late. He'd crossed a line—a line I didn't even know existed, and I no longer cared what he had to say. I rushed to the bathroom and locked the door, then messaged Lacy, asking her to come and pick me up.

Fifteen minutes later, I received a text message that read-

I'm here-

Relieved that I could finally put an end to this crazy night, I unlocked the bathroom door and rushed out to the parking lot.

That's when I realized, that in my frazzled state, I hadn't paid attention to who the notification was from, and my crazy night was far from over.

CHAPTER 6

Bones

Stitch and Wrath had a long talk with Daniels, and he'd assured them both that there was nothing going on. He made light of the fact that he and his partner had been following some of us around, saying they were just looking out for us. Cotton wanted to believe him. We all did, but something about the whole thing felt off.

Not ready to let it go, Cotton ordered Big and me to monitor the police database—not just for Daniels and Harris, but for any unusual arrests or suspicious activity. It wouldn't be hard to spot. There was little to no crime in our small town, and if there was, it was usually a simple speeding ticket or a drunk and disorderly at one of the local bars.

I understood the thought process but worried we were setting ourselves up for another wild goose chase.

Regardless, we spent the better part of the day going over all arrests that had taken place over the past two months, searching for any red flags but found nothing. I was about to start going through their work emails when there was a tap on the door, and Lacy stepped into the room. "Hey, Bones. You got a minute?"

"Yeah, what's up?"

"Elsie just called... She asked me to come to pick her up, but my car won't start." She grimaced as she asked, "Do you think you could go get her?"

It had been less than an hour since she left with her date, which left me wondering why the hell she was calling Lace for a ride. "Isn't she with her date?"

"She was, but I guess something happened."

"What do you mean something happened?"

"I don't know." Lacy shrugged. "She just sent me a message asking me to come to pick her up."

"Go get her," Big ordered. "I've got things covered here."

"You sure?"

"Yeah, I was about to call it a night anyway."

"Okay, I'll check back in with you in the morning."

"Not gonna be here. We've got the run tomorrow. We'll get back at it on Sunday."

"Sounds good."

I grabbed my things, then stood and made my way

out the door. As I started down the hall, I asked Lace, "Where is she?"

"Angelo's on the square. Just text her when you get there."

"Got it!"

I rushed out to my truck, and within seconds, I was pulling through the clubhouse gate. Concerned that Elsie might be in some kind of trouble, I hammered down on the accelerator and sped towards downtown. My mind was racing a mile a minute. I knew when that asshole showed up at the clubhouse something wasn't right about him. I figured it was just my jealousy talking, but now, I realized it was something more.

As soon as I got to the pizza place, I whipped into a parking spot at the door and messaged Elsie. My knee started bouncing as I gripped the steering wheel and stared at the front door. Relief washed over me when Elsie finally stepped outside, and I could see that she was okay. She looked surprised as she made her way over to the passenger side of my truck.

As soon as she opened the door, she said, "Hey."

"Hey."

"I thought Lacy was coming to pick me up."

"She had car trouble, so she asked me to come."

"*Yeah, I bet she did.*" She rolled her eyes as she got in and shut the door. She buckled her seat belt, then dropped her hands to the hem of her skirt, inching it down her slender thigh. "Thanks for coming to get me."

"No problem." I kept my focus on the road ahead as I asked, "There a reason why you're so anxious and your date couldn't bring you home?"

"Let's just say things didn't work out."

"I'm sorry."

"I'm not." She glanced over at me with a grimace. "He ended up being a jerk."

I can't say that I was all that disappointed that Elsie's date didn't go well. I could tell by looking at him that the guy was a douchebag, and I didn't want him anywhere near Else. Hell, I didn't want any guy around her. She was my true north. The light that guided me through the darkest shadows. The calm to my chaos. The place my mind went to whenever I needed peace. And I would do anything in my power to keep her out of harm's way.

She was all I could think about, and I wanted to make her mine.

But I loved her too much for that.

Elsie deserved someone who could give her the world—not a world of disappointment and heartbreak. She'd had enough of that to last a lifetime, and I refused to give her any more.

We were almost back to the clubhouse when Elsie

announced, "You know, we still haven't talked about the other night."

"That's because there's nothing to talk about."

"Of course, you'd say that." She turned to face me as she said, "You never want to talk about anything."

"That's not true," I argued. "I'll talk about whatever you want."

"Okay, then tell me what you were doing at the club the other night."

"I was just having a drink."

"You drove all the way into the city for a drink?"

"It wasn't exactly planned... I just needed to get away for a while."

Her eyes narrowed as she pushed, "You weren't wearing your cut."

"No, I wasn't."

"You're being intentionally vague."

"I answered your questions. What else do you want from me?"

"Nothing." She turned and stared out the window. "I don't want anything from you."

We pulled up to the clubhouse, and I'd barely gotten parked when Elsie opened her door and jumped out. I didn't move. I just sat there watching as she headed inside the clubhouse. Eventually, I got out of the truck and started after her. I was just about to reach for the door when Stitch appeared out of the darkness. There was no missing the surprise in my voice when I asked, "Hey, Pop. Where'd you come from?"

"I was out in my truck when you and Elsie pulled up." He gave me one of his looks as he said, "Figured you two might need a minute."

"Nah, not so much."

"Maybe if you'd pull your head out of your ass?"

"Maybe." I shrugged. "I'm just trying to do right by Elsie."

"Holding back isn't doing right by her."

"We both know she deserves better than me."

"*That's bullshit.* That girl would be lucky to have you."

"I wish I could believe that."

"You're the only one who doesn't." His brows furrowed, and his tone grew stern. "You gotta stop thinking you're not enough, son. You're more than enough. *You always have been.*"

Before I could open my mouth, he reached out and pulled me against him, hugging me briefly. Then, without saying anything more, he turned and headed inside the clubhouse. That was Stitch. The man who had found me all those years ago at the diner had turned into the father I never really had and the one I so desperately needed. He was a man who didn't waste words. If he said them, he meant them.

I considered his words, and deep down, I knew he was right. I was the only one standing in the way of what I wanted, and I was making a real fucking mess of things. Elsie was going on actual dates, seeing and talking to other men, and more importantly, she was growing more and more frustrated with me.

My window of opportunity with her was closing, and that rattled me.

It was at that moment that I realized my fear of losing her was stronger than my fear of not being good enough. It was that fear that had me charging into that clubhouse and down the hall to Elsie's room.

When I rounded the corner, I spotted her talking with Lace. I called out to her, and she didn't look pleased to see me. She whispered something to Lacy, and as soon as she turned to leave, Elsie started walking towards me and snapped, "What do you want, Wyatt?"

"Just a second to talk."

"I gave you a chance to talk." The fire in her eyes nearly knocked me on my ass as she sassed, "And you had nothing to say."

"You asked me crap about what happened with the asshole at the club... *Ask what you really want to ask.*"

"I don't know what you're talking about."

"*Yes, you do,*" I pushed. "Do it. Ask the question you've been wanting to ask."

The blood drained from her face, and for a

moment, I thought she was going to chicken out. After what seemed like an eternity, she finally mustered the courage to the courage to ask, "Do you like me?"

"You know I do." Her back stiffened when I added, *"That's not the question."*

"*O-kay.*" She swallowed hard, then continued, " Have you ever thought about us being together? Not as friends, but as something more."

"I have." She looked up at me with doe eyes, so full of love and hope, and all my walls started crumbling around me. I lifted my hand to her face, cupping her cheek as I trailed my thumb across her lower lip. "I think about it all the time."

Unable to resist the temptation any longer, I gently pressed my mouth against hers, feeling my world rock beneath me. I wasn't prepared for the simple touch of her lips to set me on fire, and if the little whimper that escaped her lips was any indication, she wasn't expecting it either.

Her soft, delectable lips called out to me, begging to be devoured. Our tongues met, and I became instantly addicted to her intoxicating taste. She wound her arms around my neck, and her fingers tangled in my hair as she inched even closer.

My hands drifted down her back and over the curves of her ass. Damn. I couldn't believe how incredible she felt in my arms. We were both becoming lost in the moment when Elsie placed her hands on my chest and stepped back, breaking our embrace. A light blush crept over her face as she looked up at me and whispered, "I have to go."

Before I could stop her, she turned and rushed down the hall, quickly disappearing into her room.

I didn't move.

I couldn't.

I needed to get my manhood in check before I could take a fucking step. It wasn't easy. That fucking kiss was everything I knew it would be, and it left me wanting more—much more. It's one of the many reasons why I'd waited so long to do it. Now that I had, there was no going back.

With newfound determination, I followed after her.

When I made it to her door, I stopped and took a breath.

Once I'd collected myself, I lifted my arm and was about to knock when her door flew open, and Elsie gasped, "Wyatt."

"Hey."

"Hey, I was just coming to find you." Her cheeks turned a bright shade of pink as she said, "I'm sorry. I shouldn't have just left like that. I was..."

"Go out with me," I interrupted. "I'll take you to dinner. The movies. Whatever you want."

"Umm, *ooo-kay*." She studied me for a moment, then asked, "When?"

"Tomorrow night. I'll pick you up at six." I turned and started back down the hall as I told her, "And bring a coat. It might get cold."

"I thought we were going to the movies."

"Never said we weren't... Just bring the damn coat."

And just like that, my bad day took a turn.

For five years, I'd hoped for this chance. I'd convinced myself that I wasn't the right guy for Elsie—that she deserved more than I could give her. I could still remember the harsh things my father said, and no matter how many times I was told they weren't true, there was a part of me that still believed them. It was one of the many reasons that I'd kept my distance from Elsie.

I still had my doubts, but I was going to stop holding back and let Elsie decide if I was the man she truly wanted. It was a risk. I could get my heart ripped into shreds, but for her, I was willing to take that chance.

I was going to do everything in my power to make sure I didn't fuck it up.

I was going to make our date a night to remember.

It wouldn't be easy. I didn't know much about dating, but I did know Elsie. I knew the things she liked and didn't like. I would use that to my advantage and plan a night she wouldn't soon forget.

I spent the better part of the following day getting everything ready, and while it took some work, I felt good about what I had planned. I took a shower, then put on my favorite jeans and a long sleeve t-shirt. I decided to leave my cut at home. We'd both shared a great deal of our lives with the club. I wanted this night to be just about us.

I got to the clubhouse right at six o'clock. I was feeling both nervous and excited as I made my way down the hall to her room.

I knocked, and seconds later, the door opened, and Elsie appeared with a bright smile. She looked absolutely breathtaking in her white cable-knit sweater, fitted jeans, and tall boots. Her long, red hair was down with one side pulled up in a small butterfly barrette, and it shimmered and shined just like her beautiful green eyes. "Hey."

"Hey."

"You look very handsome."

"You look incredible." A light blush swept across her cheeks as I said, "But then again, you always do."

"Well, that's not exactly true, but sweet of you to say so." Before I could argue, she reached for her coat and purse. "You ready to go?"

I nodded, then waited as she stepped out into the

hall and closed her door. I followed her down the hall and out into the parking lot. I walked over and opened the passenger side door for her, then waited for her to get settled before I closed it. I was trying to play it cool, but it wasn't easy when my heart was pounding, and my palms were sweating. I took a deep breath, then got in the truck and started the engine. "You all set?"

"I think so." She pressed her lips together, then asked, "Where exactly are we going?"

"To dinner and a movie. Just like I told you." She gave me a disapproving look—which I found adorable. "You'll see soon enough. Be patient."

"Patience isn't one of my strong suits."

"Oh, I know." I started out of the gate as I muttered, "*I know all too well.*"

I expected a rebuttal, but all I got was silence. Elsie nervously wrenched her hands in her lap for several minutes, then toyed with the latch on her purse for several more. When that didn't help, she reached over and turned on the radio. "Do you mind?"

"Not at all."

She flipped through the channels, and when she found something she liked, she smiled and sat back in her seat. The music seemed to help her relax, but her back stiffened the second she noticed that we were pulling into my driveway. "I thought we were going to have dinner?"

"We are."

I parked, then got out and walked over to Elsie's side of the truck. As I opened her door, she gave me a perplexed look. "We're going to have dinner here?"

"That's the plan."

Once she was out of the truck, I placed my palm on the small of her back and guided her up the front steps. Elsie had been to my place before, but she'd never been there alone. There was always a brother or two around, or she'd come by with the girls to grab something for Stitch. And even when she had come, it hadn't been for long.

I opened the door, and as soon as Elsie stepped inside, she tilted her head back and inhaled a deep breath. Her eyes were wide with surprise as she turned to me and asked, "You cooked?"

"I did." I closed the door behind us, then said, "You sound surprised."

"Because I am. I had no idea you could cook."

"I don't very often, but tonight is a special occasion."

"A special occasion, huh?" A smile swept across her face as she said, "I'm honored."

"As you should be."

She followed me into the kitchen and sat down at the front counter, watching as I made my way over to the stove. I'd tried my best to plan the perfect meal. I'd bought all the freshest ingredients for our roasted chicken and vegetables, but there was a slight problem. I wasn't much of a cook, but I'd rehearsed all the steps in my head and felt certain I could pull it off.

Now the time had come to prove it.

I'd already chopped the vegetables and roasted the chicken. I just needed to put together the wine sauce and check on the potatoes. As I opened the stove, Elsie asked, "Is there anything I can do to help?"

"You could get us a couple of drinks."

"Sure." She got up from her stool and started over to me. "What would you like?"

I motioned my head towards the fridge as I told her, "I've got beer for me and a bottle of wine for you."

"Perfect."

"The glasses are in the end cabinet."

She nodded, then walked over to the fridge and took out a Miller Lite. She placed it on the counter next to me before grabbing a glass from the cabinet. I continued making the sauce while she opened the bottle and poured herself a glass of wine. After she put the bottle back in the fridge, she went back over and sat down. "It smells really good."

"Hopefully, it'll taste good, too."

"I'm sure it will be great."

Once I had everything ready, Elsie helped me carry it to the kitchen table, and we both fixed ourselves a plate. I waited for Elsie to take the first bite, and to my profound relief, she smiled and said, "Wow. This is really good."

"I'm glad you like it." I took a quick bite, and I was pleasantly surprised to discover that she wasn't exaggerating. It really was good. Silence fell upon us as we both continued to eat. I didn't mind the quiet. I was used to it, but I couldn't help but notice how Elsie's eyes were skirting around the room and the way she was shifting in her seat. It was clear that she was troubled by our lack of conversation, so I asked, "So, what did Lace and the girls say about us going out tonight?"

"What do you mean?"

"Oh, come on. I'm sure they had plenty to say."

"Yeah, you could say that." She shrugged with a smirk. "But I could never repeat what they said. That would be a breach of trust."

"Hmmm, I see."

"But I will say, they were all pretty curious why you waited until now to ask me out. So was I, actually. I mean, we've known each other for six years. Why now?"

"I guess you could say I finally came to my senses... I just hope I'm not too late."

CHAPTER 7
Elsie

My mother told me never to settle. She assured me that there was someone out there who would be the answer to all my prayers. She said to wait for the man who was willing to see me through rough patches, laugh with me, cry with me, and most of all, fight for me. And that man would love me in the way that I deserved.

She said I would know when I found him, and she was right. I did know.

I knew the day Wyatt gave me that journal that he was the man my mother had told me about. I'd been waiting five years for him to realize it, too, but I knew in my heart that he was worth the wait.

Like they say, 'the longer the wait, the sweeter the kiss.' As far as I was concerned, no truer words had ever been spoken.

I reached across the table and placed my hand on his as I told him, "You're not too late."

"Glad to hear that."

He held my gaze for a moment, then we both turned our attention back to our dinner. When we finished eating, I helped Wyatt clear the table, and once we had everything put away, Wyatt grabbed our coats from the entryway, then asked, "You ready?"

"Sure."

I thought we were about to head to the movies, but instead, Wyatt led me outside to his backyard. I had no idea what we were doing until I saw all the little white lights and the fire. Not only had he strung lights from every tree, but he'd also set up a movie screen and a projector. It was the most romantic thing I'd ever seen. As I gazed at all the twinkling white lights and the flickering fire, I whispered, "Oh, Wyatt. This is so beautiful."

"You like it?"

"I love it." I followed him over to the fire, and once I was seated, Wyatt offered me a blanket and a fresh glass of wine. "I can't believe you did all this."

"I wanted to do something special for you."

"Well, you definitely did that."

A proud smirk crossed his face as he walked over and started setting up the projector. As soon as the *Lost Boys* appeared on the screen, I gasped, "You didn't!"

"It's one of your favorites, right?"

"It is!" I looked at the screen, then back at him. "I can't believe you remembered."

"It wasn't all that hard. It's one of my favorites, too."

Once he had everything the way he wanted it, he came over and sat down next to me. He tossed one of the blankets over him, then nestled back in his chair. Even though we'd both seen the movie many times before, the flickering light of the fire and the twinkling of the little white lights made it feel like it was the first time.

We talked a little bit, shared our favorite moments of the movie and discussed other movies we wanted to see in the future, but mostly, we just sat back and enjoyed watching our favorite movie together.

When it was over, I helped him take down the screen, and we carried everything inside. I was waiting for him to finish putting everything away in the closet when I told him, "I really enjoyed the movie."

"I did, too. We'll have to do it again sometime."

"I'd like that."

He closed the closet, then turned to face me as he asked, "You ready to head back?"

It was late, but I'd had such an amazing night with him, and I wasn't ready for it to end. I wasn't sure how to tell him that, so I simply shook my head no.

He studied me for a moment, and like he could read my mind, he stepped closer and slipped his arm behind my back, inching me closer. Desire flashed through his eyes, and I knew the moment had finally come.

He was finally going to kiss me again.

I held my breath as he lowered his mouth to mine. His rough hands slid across my skin with reverence and possessiveness like I'd never known, and I could literally feel his passion pouring into me as he deepened the kiss. His fingertips twisted into my hair as he raked his teeth across my bottom lip, nipping me lightly.

And just like that, I was hit with a whirlwind of heat and desire, and I had to hold onto him to keep myself from becoming lost in a delicious haze of hormones and lust. Being in his arms was everything I'd imagined it would be and more. The more turned on I became, the more I imagined all the wicked things he could do to me.

His lips on my neck.

His greedy hands on my body.

The pleasure-filled orgasms he'd give me over and over again.

It wasn't like me to have such thoughts—not like these, but it felt so good to have his mouth on mine, and I couldn't get enough.

A wanton groan slipped through my lips as I

inched closer, pressing my body against his. I'd never felt so consumed with need. I wanted him so much—more than I ever dreamed possible, and if his touch was any indication, he felt the same about me. Things were quickly getting heated, and I had a feeling they were only going to get more heated—which made me a little nervous.

It was only our first date. I wasn't ready to take that step with him, so I placed my palms on his broad, muscular chest and gave him a gentle push as I stepped back, breaking our embrace. Concern flashed through his eyes as he asked, "Something wrong?"

"No... maybe," I stammered. "It's just a little fast."

"We've known each other for six years. I wouldn't say that's exactly fast."

"We've known each other, but we've never even been on a date before tonight. This is all new, and I don't want to mess things up by moving too fast."

"I get it." He leaned in and gave me a quick kiss on the temple. "We can take things at whatever speed you want."

"Thank you, Wyatt. I appreciate that."

"I guess I should be getting you back."

"Okay."

He waited as I collected my things, then led me out to his truck. And just like that, our date was over, and we were headed back to the clubhouse. I glanced over at Wyatt, and just looking at his handsome face had me second-guessing my decision to take things slow. It was too late to do anything about it now, so I sighed and turned my attention to the road ahead.

"You okay over there?"

"Yeah, I'm good," I lied. "Just a little tired."

"Hope I didn't keep you out too late."

"No, not at all. I had a wonderful time, and I'm sad it had to end."

"Well, how 'bout we go do something tomorrow night?"

"What would you want to do?"

"I'm up for anything. We could go to the city, or we could just hang at my place again. Whatever you want."

"Either would be great. I honestly don't care what we do, so you choose."

"Okay, we'll figure out something."

When we got to the clubhouse, Wyatt led me inside, and to my surprise, we didn't see any of the brothers as we walked down the hall to my room. I opened my door and thought he'd follow me inside, but he remained fixed in the doorway. "I best be going."

"Okay." The thought of him leaving made my heart ache a little. "Good night."

"Night."

With that, he brought his hands to my face, gently cupping his palms along my jaw as he lowered his lips to mine, kissing me passionately. God. He felt so good, smelled so good, and I couldn't help but let myself get swept away.

I let my hands roam over the perfectly defined muscles of his chest, then around to his back as I inched closer. I felt so safe in his arms, like nothing in the world could harm me as long as he was holding me close. Just as I was melting into his arms, he released my mouth and said, "I'll see you tomorrow."

I stood there, lost in a blissful haze, as Wyatt turned and made his way back down the hall. Once he was out of sight, I stepped into my room and closed the door. I was still floating on Cloud 9 as I slipped on my pajamas and curled into bed. I closed my eyes, but there was no way I was going to get any sleep. My mind was swimming with thoughts about Wyatt.

The sexy curve of his lips when he smiled, the spark in his eyes when he looked at me, and most of all, the feel of his lips on mine. Every breath I took brought on another thought or memory, and there was nothing I could do to stop it. And I wasn't so sure I wanted to. I liked the way I felt when I was with him.

I spent hours staring at the ceiling, reliving every moment I'd shared with him, and before I knew it, the sun was starting to rise. I didn't do well with no sleep, so I laid there for another hour or so, hoping I might doze off. Sadly, all I did was toss and turn, so I got out of bed and headed into the bathroom for a shower.

Just as I feared, I was tired and grumpy. I hoped that the hot water would help, but no such luck. I was just as irritable when I got out and dried off. I managed to get dressed without any issues, but I had no desire to put on makeup or fix my hair. I just threw on a baseball cap, then headed to the kitchen for coffee and a bite to eat.

When I walked in, Lacy and the girls were gathered around the stove, making breakfast for the guys. At first, they didn't notice that I'd entered the room and was pouring myself a cup of coffee, but the second Lacy spotted me, she shrieked, "There you are! I was beginning to think you would never get up!"

"It's not even eight o'clock."

"Yeah, well, we've been up since six." Lacy followed me over to the table and sat down next to me. "How did it go last night?"

"It was good. I had a nice time."

"A nice time?" She gave me a nudge with her elbow. "Come on, woman! You gotta give me more than that."

"I don't have much more to give."

"Why?" Concern marked her face as she asked, "Did something happen? Was he an asshole?"

"No, nothing like that. I'm just really tired. I didn't get much sleep."

"Didn't get much sleep, huh?" A mischievous smirk swept across her face as she teased, "Does that mean he finally deflowered you?"

"Deflowered me? What planet are you from?" I gave her an annoyed glare. "I can't deal with you today."

"Oh, come on. You know I'm just messing with you." She gave me a nudge with her elbow, then shook her head with a grumble. "You are such a grumpy pants when you don't get enough sleep."

"I know. I just can't seem to help myself."

"It's fine. I'm the same way when I've had a long night," she replied, sounding disappointed. "But everything went okay? You had a good time with him?"

"I had a great time with him." I took a sip of my coffee, then smiled. "I'm hoping I'll have another great time tonight."

"Tonight?" She leaned in closer. "You're going out again tonight?"

"We are."

"So, *things did go well last night.*"

"Very much so."

"Well, it's about damn time. I knew you two would hit it off." Lacy's smile widened. "And if you wanna keep hitting it off, you best get your tired ass back to your room and get some sleep 'cause I highly doubt Bones is gonna want to spend his night with Ms. Crabby Patty."

"You're right, but I'm wound too tight to sleep."

"We could go for a run or head into town and carb out on some pancakes."

"Hmmm... Pancakes sound like heaven."

"Then, let's go load up."

I was starving and the mere thought of a big plate of pancakes had my mouth watering, so I needed no further persuasion. I followed her out of the kitchen, and we raced out to her car. Seconds later, we were headed towards town. We hadn't been riding long when I remembered how Wyatt picked me up from my date. "Hey, I thought there was something wrong with your car."

"Huh?"

"Wyatt said it wouldn't start. It was why he came to pick me up the other night."

"Oh, that." Lacy grimaced. "I might've lied about that."

"What? Why would..." My head fell back as I groaned. "You did it so he'd come and pick me up."

"Guilty as charged."

"I guess I should thank you. If you hadn't lied, then Wyatt would've never asked me out."

"Oh, he would've asked you out on his own eventually, but I didn't see any harm in giving him another little push."

"Well, thank you for looking out for me."

"That's what friends are for."

When we got to the diner, Lacy parked, and we raced inside. The smell of maple syrup and butter filled the air as we made our way over to one of the tables in the back. We placed our orders, then waited as the waitress brought over our drinks. Once she'd gone back to the kitchen, Lacy leaned towards me and asked, "So, what about the guy from your class? You never told me why you cut the date short."

"He ended up being a total douchebag. He said some pretty nasty stuff about the brothers, and I just couldn't stand to sit there and listen to it."

"I don't blame you there. There's nothing worse than suffering through a bad date." She chuckled as she asked, "Did I ever tell you about the time I went out with a so-called 'artist'?"

"No, I don't believe I've ever heard about him."

"Really? I can't believe I never told you. He was awful." She looked mortified as she told me, "He took me to this really nice restaurant, and then for some asinine reason, he thought it was acceptable to paint a grand 'masterpiece' right there on the wall! And to make matters worse, it was awful. It looked like a three-year-old had thrown finger paints on the wall."

"That's truly awful, Lacy. I don't know what I would've done."

"I did the only thing I could. I pretended like I had no idea who he was and bolted. The idiot didn't even know I'd left."

"That's awful." I was still giggling when the waitress brought over our food. "As bad as that was, I think I have you beat. I went out with a guy who thought it was okay to talk about his ex the entire night. He wouldn't stop going on and on about how much he missed her and how she was the best thing that ever happened to him. I wanted to crawl under the table."

We both burst out laughing and continued to eat our pancakes. We spent the rest of the meal talking about other crazy dates we'd been on, and all in all, it was just what I needed. As soon as we got back to the clubhouse, I went to my room and got into bed, then spent the next couple of hours sleeping like a baby.

When I woke up, my bad mood had lifted, and I was feeling excited about my date with Wyatt. I took another shower and changed into something more appropriate for a date. It was a bit chilly out, so I decided to wear a sweater with jeans and boots. I put on a little makeup, and I was about to straighten my hair when there was a knock at my door. "Just a minute!"

I didn't want to hold him up, so I grabbed one of

my clips and pulled my hair up into a messy twist. I gave myself one last quick look in the mirror, then rushed over to answer the door. When I opened it, I found Wyatt standing in the hall. Like the night before, he wasn't wearing his cut or biker boots. He was simply wearing jeans with a white t-shirt and an old letterman's jacket, and he looked so damn hot.

I couldn't imagine him looking more handsome until he gave me one of his lopsided grins and said, "I'm a little early."

"That's okay. I was ready." I reached for my purse and asked, "So, where are we going?"

"I thought we could go back to my place and order a couple of pizzas. Maybe watch the game or a movie?"

"Sounds great to me."

I grabbed my coat and followed him out to his truck. He opened my door and waited as I got inside. As soon as I was settled, he leaned down and lowered his mouth to mine, kissing me briefly. "You look beautiful tonight."

"I'm glad you think so."

He looked at me for a moment, then without saying anything more, he closed the door and walked over to his side of the truck. Once he was inside next to me, he started the truck, and we were on our way to his place. Neither of us spoke, but it wasn't an awkward silence.

That's how it was with Wyatt. There was no pressure to speak or try to impress. He didn't need to fill the void with nonsense, and I liked that about him.

When we got to his house, Wyatt led me inside and offered me a drink. "You want wine or a beer? I've got tea and soda, too."

"A beer would be good."

"You got it." He walked over to the fridge and pulled out two Ultra's, then offered one to me. "What kind of pizza would you like?"

Before I could answer, there was a knock on the door. Wyatt looked surprised as he grumbled, "What the hell?"

He walked over, and as soon as he opened the door, Savage and Wrath stepped inside, each carrying a twelve-pack of beer. Savage glanced over in the living room as he asked, "You got the game on?"

"Not yet."

"Well, what are you waiting for?" Savage started towards the kitchen, but stopped the second he spotted me standing in the doorway. "Whoa. Are we interrupting something?"

"Yeah, you could say that," Wyatt answered.

"Well damn, brother. Why didn't you say something?"

"Like you gave me a chance."

"Well, shit. We didn't mean to barge in on ya."

Savage looked over to Wrath as he said, "Guess we can watch it at the clubhouse."

"You don't have to do that." It was no secret that they were all big Lakers fans and usually watched the game together. I hated to mess up their plan, so I suggested, "We can all watch it together."

"You sure?"

"Absolutely." I glanced over at Wyatt as I asked Savage, "Are you guys hungry? We were just about to order some pizza."

"Hell yeah." Savage nodded. "Yeah, grab us a couple of supremes and a large order of wings."

He put their beer in the fridge, then rushed over to join Wrath on the sofa. Without waiting for us to join, Wrath turned on the TV and started searching for the game. Wyatt let out a breath, then stepped over to me and whispered, "I'm sorry. I had no idea they were coming."

"It's fine. Don't worry about it." I glanced back at the boys, chuckling when I saw them giving each other a high five. "It's gonna be fun."

"Thanks for being so understanding." He leaned in and kissed me on the forehead. "You go make yourself comfortable, and I'll order the pizzas."

I nodded, then carried my beer into the living room and sat down on the loveseat. After Wyatt placed our order, he came over and sat down next to me. At first, Savage and Wrath were too wrapped up in the game to even notice that we were sitting across from them, but as soon as a commercial break came on, Savage turned his focus to us.

He looked at Wyatt and then over to me. He raised his hand and motioned it between us as he asked, "So, what's this about? You two finally making a go of it?"

"Don't start with that shit," Wyatt fussed.

"What? It's a legitimate question," he replied innocently. "Fuck's sake. You two have been playing cat and mouse for years. You can't blame us for wondering."

Wyatt didn't respond. He just sat there glaring a hole through Savage. I thought his silence would put an end to the conversation, but I was wrong. It only added fuel to the fire. "Well, if you two are sticking to the whole *'we're just friends'* bullshit, then you shouldn't care if I ask Elsie out myself."

"And what makes you think I'd say yes?"

"You'd be a fool not to." He turned to me with an arrogant smirk. "You know I'd show you a real good time."

"That's enough, Savage. It's never gonna happen."

"And why's that?"

"Because Elsie's mine," Wyatt growled. "She always has been."

I wasn't sure what to make of Wyatt's declaration. A part of me felt relieved and excited by the thought that he thought of me as his, but there was another part of me that felt annoyed that I hadn't had some kind of say in the matter. It was that part of me that had me standing up and storming out of the room.

I went into the kitchen, and I was about to go to the fridge for a cold beer when Wyatt came into the room. "Is something wrong?"

"No," I lied.

"You sure about that?"

"Um-hmm. Everything's perfectly fine." I crossed my arms as I grumbled, "I have no qualms about you announcing to your brothers that I'm yours and always have been. I mean, it would've been nice to have some kind of discussion about what's going on with us beforehand, but whatever."

"So, you are mad." He stepped over to me and placed his hands on my hips. "The last thing I wanted to do was upset you. I thought you knew where I stood."

"So, what you said was true?" I forced myself to look him in the eye as I asked, "You want me?"

"How can you ask that?" Seeing the swirl of emotion in his eyes as he stood there staring at me stole my breath. "Of course, I want you. I always have."

When he pulled me close, I swallowed, holding my breath as I waited for him to lower his mouth to mine. Just before his lips touched mine, he paused. His dark eyes fell on me, searching for some kind of confirmation that I wanted this as much as he did, and when he found what he was looking for, his mouth crashed against mine. The second our lips touched, I became consumed with emotion. I didn't question it. I didn't let my worries of inadequacies sneak into the back of my mind. Instead, I let myself go.

I was there with him—the place I was always meant to be.

CHAPTER 8
Bones

I'd planned to take things slow. It's what she needed. It's what she'd asked for, but the woman was driving me to the brink of insanity. The simple touch of her lips set me on fire, an intense heat surging throughout my body. Her soft, delectable lips called out to me, begging to be devoured. Our tongues met, and I became instantly addicted to her intoxicating taste—sweet warmth with a hint of mint.

A light moan vibrated through her chest as her fingers began tangling in my hair. She pressed her breasts against my chest as my hands roamed down her back and over the curves of her ass. I couldn't believe how perfect she felt in my arms. It was like she was made for me and only me.

Remembering the guys were just in the next room, I pulled back, but when I looked down at her lust-filled eyes, I couldn't stop myself from leaning in for another. She opened her mouth with a low moan, and I couldn't stop myself from delving deeper, savoring the soft caress of her lips and the quickening of her breath. Just like the times before, I quickly became lost in her touch, unable to control the storm of desire that was brewing deep inside of me.

I was on the verge of scooping her into my arms and carrying her to my bed when I heard Savage shout, "There's no way he could've missed that fucking foul! Where the fuck did they get these refs?"

"Come on! That's bullshit!" Wrath roared.

Amidst all the shouting and carrying on, the doorbell rang, and Elsie giggled when Savage yelled, "Bones! The pizza is here!"

"Coming!" I hated that we'd been interrupted, but there was little I could do about it. I brought my hand up to Elsie's face, then softly raked my knuckles along her cheek. "I'll get rid of them."

"No, you don't have to do that." She raked her teeth across her bottom lip. "It's fine. Besides, the game won't last *that* long."

"You sure?"

She nodded, then said, "Positive."

The doorbell rang again, and Wrath immediately started shouting, "Yo! Bones! The pizza..."

"I said I was coming!"

Elsie followed me back into the living room and returned to her spot on the loveseat while I answered the door. I'd barely given the driver his cash when Savage and Wrath came rushing up behind me. They greedily grabbed the boxes of pizza and carried them over to the table. Wrath opened one of the boxes, and they were about to dive in when I told them, "You know, I've got plates."

"Yeah, my bad."

Wrath sat down, and they waited as I went to the kitchen to grab some napkins and plates. When I returned, we all loaded up on pizza and wings, then sat back and watched the game. Every so often, I would glance over at Elsie, and time and time again, I found her staring at me with a heated look in her eyes. Seeing that she wanted me just as much as I wanted her had my cock throbbing against my jeans.

I wanted nothing more than to toss her over my shoulder and carry her to my bedroom, but with the guys sitting right next to us, that wasn't an option. So, I did the only thing I could. I sat back and watched the game, biding my time until Elsie and I were finally alone.

It was a tough game, but in the end, the Lakers won. The guys were feeling the need to celebrate, so I wasn't surprised when Savage suggested, "We should head down to Danvers and play a couple of rounds of pool."

"I'm in." Wrath finished off his beer, then stood and started for the door. "You two coming?"

"No. I think we're gonna pass."

"Seriously?"

"Yeah, seriously."

Savage studied me for a moment, then shrugged and mumbled, "Okay. Suit yourself."

Without any further argument, Wrath and Savage said their goodbyes to Elsie and then, they were on their way. They'd barely walked out when Elsie hopped up and started collecting all the empty pizza boxes. "I can get that later."

"It's no problem."

She didn't even look at me as she skirted past me and headed into the kitchen. I grabbed a few empty bottles from the table, then followed her into the kitchen. I tossed the empty beers into the trash and was about to walk over to Elsie when she darted into the living room for more trash.

When she returned, I couldn't help but notice that the heated look in her eyes from earlier was gone and had been replaced with a look of apprehension. Curious about what was going on with her, I asked, "Hey, is everything okay?"

"Yes... No." She tossed everything into the trash,

then whipped around to face me. "This is just our second date."

"Yeah. And?"

"I really love being with you, and I don't want to mess it up."

"You're worrying over nothing, Elsie. There's nothing you could do that would ever mess this up."

"I wish that was true, but it's not."

"I don't understand."

I felt like I was punched in the gut when she admitted, "I know about you and Lacy... And Makayla and the other hang arounds."

I didn't have to ask. I knew exactly what she was talking about.

There was a time when I thought I'd never be with a woman. I was socially awkward and quiet. I didn't know how to talk to a beautiful woman, much less how to pleasure them, so I kept my distance. But the girls made it their mission to pull me out of my shell, and after one too many drinks, I found myself in bed with Makayla.

She made it easy. She was eager and experienced, so there was no question of what I should do. Makayla took control, and in a blink, my cock was in her mouth, and I was about to blow. I'd barely come when I was eager for more, and Makayla was quick to give me what I wanted. After that night, I stopped being distant with Makayla. In fact, I pursued her on countless occasions, but no matter how intense, how rough or taboo, I always felt like there was something missing.

I spent a few random nights with Lacy and a couple of the other hang arounds, but like I had with Makayla, I was often left feeling unfulfilled. It was all in my head. I knew that, but I quickly lost interest in getting an easy lay. I wanted something more. I wanted Elsie.

I stepped over to her and did my best to keep my voice steady as I told her, "I don't know what they told you, but that was a long time ago. I haven't hooked up with any of them in years."

"I know. That's not the issue."

"Then, what is?" I gave her a moment, but she didn't respond. "I can't read minds, Elsie. You gotta talk to me, or we're never gonna get past this."

"I'm not Lacy or the other girls."

"Not seeing how that's a problem."

"I don't have the experience they have." Her eyes met mine as she admitted, "I have some, but nothing like them."

"Wait... Are you saying..."

"Yeah, that's exactly what I'm saying."

Once again, I felt like the wind had been knocked out of me.

I don't know why I was surprised by her confession. Elsie had made a point never to mess around with any of the brothers. Hell, she'd hurt their feelings in a second if one of them crossed a line, and she was the same way with the assholes from her school. I always knew the dates never led to anything, but I never dreamed that she'd never been intimate with a man.

The thought of her being untouched, unmarked by another man, fascinated me in ways I couldn't begin to describe. I wasn't bothered at all. In fact, it only made me want her more. "How can you think that's a problem?"

"It's not a problem exactly." She placed the palm of her hand on my chest as she said, "It's just we've finally gotten to this point, and I really like the way things are going. I don't want to do anything that might mess things up."

"That could never happen, but if you're worried about it, we'll take things slow."

"That's just it. I don't want to take things slow." She slipped her arms around my neck and pulled me close as she whispered, "I want to be with you. I really do. I'm just..."

"I get it. I really do." I kept my eyes trained on hers as I said, "I need you to tell me something."

"*O-kay.*"

"How many dates would it take?"

She lowered her hands and stepped back with a confused expression. "What do you mean?"

"How many dates would it take?"

"It's not about that, Wyatt."

"I don't want you doing anything until you're ready, and if that means we go on a couple more dates, then that's what we'll do."

"Or..." She reached for my hand and led me down the hall. "We could just take things a little slow now and see how it goes."

As soon as we were in the bedroom, she turned to face me, slipped her arms around my neck, and drew me close. Without giving me a chance to argue, her lips met mine in an explosive kiss, so eager and full of hunger, and every touch of her tongue only made my need grow more intense. She felt so fucking incredible. Hell, it was all I could do to keep myself from taking her right there standing in the bedroom door.

My tongue glided along hers, stoking the fire that burned deep within us both. Fisting her hair at the nape of her neck, I eased her head back, and delved my tongue deeper into her mouth. Arching against me, she moaned when I broke the kiss and began trailing my lips along her jawline, licking my way down her neck.

"You're so fucking incredible." Nibbling on her

lobe, I ran the tip of my tongue along the length of her neck, then made my way back to her mouth.

All her little whimpers and moans spurred me on, guiding me to give her exactly what she needed.

There was nothing else like it.

When I finally drew back, she looked up at me with lust-filled eyes, and I knew I had to have her. Resting my forehead against hers, I stared into her eyes. "I need you to be sure about this."

"I am sure." Her eyes filled with emotion as she whispered, "I trust you, Wyatt. I know you won't hurt me."

"Fuck."

I placed my hand at the nape of her neck, drawing her close once again. She ran her fingers through my hair, pulling me closer, and returning my kiss with fervor. A part of me had always known that the pull I felt towards her was mutual. I could feel it lingering under the surface, just begging to be released, and if this kiss was any indication, there was no doubt that Elsie wanted me just as much as I wanted her.

My hands moved lower, exploring her body, and she moaned into my mouth as I grabbed her ass and pulled her closer. I felt a slight smile play on her lips as she ground her hips against mine, clearly enjoying my growing arousal. My cock throbbed against the fabric between us, aching to be buried between her legs.

I gave Elsie's hair another slight tug, forcing her head back as I trailed my lips down her throat. Her breath caught as I reached the dip between her neck and collarbone. Her hands gripped my hair, and I could feel her heart hammering in her chest.

I couldn't remember ever wanting anything like I wanted her. For reasons I couldn't begin to explain, I needed her, burned for her, and with every touch, she stoked the fucking fire. She shifted her hips forward, grinding herself against my ever-hardening cock. I looked down at her as I warned, "We start this, then there's no going back. I'm going to want you again and again."

She rocked against me, taunting me to give her what she so desperately desired, and with one last shift of her hips, all of our inhibitions disintegrated into the darkness. I stepped forward, pinning her back against the wall, then trailed kisses to her earlobe.

I wanted to take things slow, but Elsie's soft sighs fueled my desire. I needed more.

More of her little whimpers.

More of her intoxicating scent.

More of her touch.

I wanted to explore every inch of her body. It was at that moment that I realized how different I felt with Elsie than with the others. I didn't feel that sense of emptiness in the pit of my stomach. It was just the opposite. I felt whole. Alive. Recharged in a way that I'd never felt before, and it was all her.

Elsie was my reset.

I ran my tongue along the curve of her neck as she moaned, "Oh, Wyatt."

Unable to resist a moment longer, her hands slid down my chest to the hem of my t-shirt. A sexy smirk crept across her lips as she lifted it over my head and tossed it to the floor. Her pupils grew wide as her gaze burned across my muscular chest and various tattoos. If the expression on her face was any indication, she liked what she saw.

Elsie took a step back and slowly slipped off her boots, then her sweater and jeans. She looked absolutely stunning standing there in only her white lace bra and panties. Her eyes remained fixed on mine as she placed her hands on her hips, then slowly eased her panties down her hips. As soon as they hit the floor, she reached behind her back and unfastened her bra.

The second she slipped it from her shoulders, I took a step forward and pinned her against the wall. "So fucking beautiful."

I needed to make sure she was ready for me, so I lowered my hand between her legs. I slid my fingers across her center and was pleased to find that she was already wet for me. With my other hand, I cupped her breast, brushing the pad of my thumb over her hard nipple. I kissed along the curve of her neck as I started to tease her clit.

I began trailing kisses along her collarbone, then slowly made my way down her stomach as I lifted her left thigh and hooked it over my shoulder. I glanced up at her as I asked, "You still trust me?"

She nodded, then watched as I brushed the tips of my fingers up and down her center, then slipped a finger inside and kneaded her clit with my thumb. She moaned as she rode my fingers, and by the sound of her rapid breaths, I could tell she was getting close. I moved my mouth to her clit, nipping and sucking as my fingers continued their torturous rhythm.

"I... I'm... I'm... Oh, God! Don't stop," she cried out, her fingernails digging into my shoulders, desperate for something to hold on to. Twisting her fingers in my hair, she succumbed to her release. She continued to chant curses as she fell into the haze of her release.

Her body grew limp, but I wasn't done with her yet—*not even close.*

CHAPTER 9
Elsie

Being with Wyatt was nothing like I'd ever experienced before.

Every fevered look, every touch, every kiss had me begging for more.

He'd just given me an earth-shattering orgasm when he stood and faced me. He slipped his arms around my waist, then pulled me close. There was a fierce look in his eyes, one that sent a chill down my spine, and I knew then he wasn't done with me.

No. He was just getting started.

He brushed his lips against mine, but not gently like before. Instead, it was hot, passionate, and demanding, and I loved it. I moaned into his mouth, stealing the last of his restraint.

He leaned down and lifted me up, cradling me close to his chest as he carried me over to the bed. He held me tightly, making me feel safe and secure in his arms. Seconds later, I was on my back and his body covered mine. His weight pressed me into the bed as his hands, rough and impatient, roamed over my body. His touch felt so good, so right, and I only wanted more.

He kissed me, soft and tender, then looked down at me and waited until I gave him a nod, letting him know that I was okay to move forward. He waited a moment, giving me a chance to change my mind, then lifted off of me and started taking off his jeans. I watched in awe as he lowered them down his hips. He was beautiful. From his perfectly chiseled chest to his exquisitely pronounced V, he was a sight to behold.

The man was truly beautiful.

Before tossing his jeans to the floor, he took out his wallet and began searching for a condom. Once he found one, he slipped it on, then looked down at me sprawled out on the bed. "You're amazing, Elsie. Absolutely amazing."

I continued to watch with eagerness as he lowered himself back down on the bed. He hovered over me for a moment, looking into my eyes with one of his soul-searching stares, then he slowly positioned himself between my legs. I inhaled a quick breath when he raked his cock against me.

I knew what was coming. I knew there was a

chance that it would be painful, but I didn't care. I was so lost in the moment that all I could think about was the all-consuming need I felt for him. He reached between us, then centered himself as he said, "I'm going to go slow, but I can't promise that it won't hurt a little."

"I'm good... Don't stop."

He nodded, then slowly inched forward. I felt a slight sting, but not enough to take away from the moment. I just needed a second to acclimate myself. After a couple of deep breaths, I placed my hands on his chest and slowly began to move, matching the rhythm as I rocked my hips against him.

Bliss. Pure bliss. I had no idea it could be so good, and I wanted to savor the moment. I wanted to let myself feel every erotic sensation. But Wyatt had other plans.

A deep growl vibrated through his chest as his pace quickened, becoming more demanding and intense with each shift of his hips. The muscles in my abdomen began to tighten and without thinking, my legs drew up beside him. My fingers grasped his biceps as I held on to him, bracing myself for the next wave of pleasure that crashed through my body.

With one deep thrust, my orgasm jolted through me, and I was left shocked and shuddering from the intense pleasure. I was completely spent, but he didn't stop. Not even close. He drove into me again and again until he found his own release, growling out like a satisfied bear as he lowered his body onto mine. I lay there limp beneath him, listening silently to the rapid beating of his heart. Just as it began to slow, Wyatt eased off of me and rolled over on his side.

After a couple of deep breaths, he disposed of the condom, then slipped his arm under me and pulled me close. I laid my head on his chest and sighed. He immediately turned to me with concern in his eyes. "Are you okay? Did I hurt you?"

"No, I'm good."

"You're sure?" he asked with concern. "You don't need anything?"

"I'm fine, Wyatt." I gave him a warm smile. "In fact, I'm more than fine. I had no idea it would be like that."

"Like what?"

"*Like that*. It was incredible."

"Yes, it was."

While I was relieved that he'd agreed, I was curious to know if he thought things had gone as well as I thought they had. I leaned up on my elbow and tried to be casual as I asked, "Are you sure about that? Was it really okay?"

"It was more than okay, Elsie." He eased forward

and kissed me on the temple. "You had nothing to worry about."

"Good."

I laid back on the pillow and inched up the covers as I curled up next to him. We lay there quietly for several minutes, and I was beginning to think Wyatt had drifted off to sleep until he asked, "Are you tired?"

"Not really."

"Me either." He sat up in bed and asked, "Do you want to watch TV or something?"

"Yeah, that sounds good."

He nodded, then got up and collected his boxers from the floor. When he started to get dressed, I eased out of bed and gathered my clothes from the floor. I was about to go get cleaned up when Wyatt said, "Just a second."

I waited and watched as he walked over to his dresser and pulled out a long sleeve t-shirt and a pair of plaid boxers. He tossed it over to me as he said, "This might be more comfortable."

"Thanks."

With clothes in hand, I darted into the bathroom and cleaned up a bit; then, I put on the clothes Wyatt had given me. I gave myself a quick check in the mirror, and after fixing my smudged eyeliner, I opened the door and stepped back into the bedroom. There was no sign of Wyatt, so I started down the hall and called out, "Wyatt?"

"I'm in the kitchen." When I walked in, I found him standing in front of the refrigerator wearing only his boxer briefs and a wife-beater t-shirt, and he looked unbelievably sexy. A soft smile crept across his handsome face as his eyes skirted over me. "I like the look."

"Thanks." I could feel the warmth of my blush as it crept along my cheeks. "I like yours, too."

"Glad you like it... You hungry?"

Wrath and Savage had wiped out most of the pizza and wings, so I didn't get much to eat. And after our little workout, I had a little grumble in my stomach. "Umm, yeah. I could eat. Whatcha got?"

"Not a lot." He searched a moment longer, then said, "I can make us an omelet or a grilled cheese? Or an egg sandwich?"

"Oooh, an egg sandwich sounds good."

"Yeah, it does."

He pulled out the eggs and mayo and placed them on the counter, then he took out a skillet. It was strange seeing him like this—so relaxed and laidback. It was almost like I was getting a secret glimpse of his life outside of the club—one that no one else got to see. Enthralled, I sat down on the stool and watched him fry our eggs.

When they were almost done, he pulled out the

bread and started to spread mayonnaise on each slice. As soon as he was done, he stepped back over to the stove to check on the eggs. That's when I told him, "My mother used to make egg sandwiches whenever my brother and I were sick- like every single time. Earache. Stomachache. Egg sandwich. I swear she thought they had special healing powers."

"I would never think about eating an egg when I was a kid. Just the thought of them turned my stomach." He cut each of the sandwiches into triangles as he told me, "But Stitch ate them all the time, and I was determined to be just like him, so I gave it a go. Turns out, they weren't so bad. I even grew to like them."

"Don't take this the wrong way, but when I first moved to the clubhouse, I was completely terrified of your dad."

Wyatt slid my plate over to me as he snickered, "He does make quite a first impression."

"He certainly does. He makes a pretty impactful second and third impression, too," I giggled. "But now that I've gotten to know him, I'm still pretty terrified of him."

"Really? Why? He's just a big teddy bear."

"Stitch is nothing of the sort. He's more like a rabid bear or a starved mountain lion or a werewolf on a full moon."

"I get it. He's a big scary dude, but he was more of

a father to me than my ol' man ever was. He saw me for me. Never treated me like I was just some weird kid. He didn't call me names or put me down. He took the time to get to know me, and that meant something to me. It still does."

"I'm glad you have him in your life."

"Me, too. I don't know what I would've done without him."

"Do you think you would've joined the MC if he hadn't come around?"

"No, probably not, but then, there's a lot of things I wouldn't have done if it hadn't been for him."

"Like what?"

"Rebuilding an engine. Riding a motorcycle. Going to a party and getting hammered." He shrugged. "The brothers got me to do stuff I never thought I'd do."

"They can be pretty persuasive."

"That's an understatement," he chuckled. "But honestly, when I was younger, I didn't need a lot of persuading. I wanted to do the things they were doing, even if it was something I was skeptical about. I guess the draw to being like them was stronger than my fear of failing."

I'd known Wyatt for over two years before I discovered that he had Asperger's. I wouldn't have known then if he hadn't told me. I'd always just thought he was quiet and reserved, but as we got closer, he started opening up to me about the struggles he'd had growing up and how he still struggled with his temper. I liked that he felt comfortable enough to talk to me about the struggles he'd had.

It made me feel closer to him, and I wanted that more now than ever. "I wish I had known you when you were younger. I bet you were adorable."

"What? You don't think I'm adorable now?"

"Oh, you're plenty adorable, especially when you cook in your boxers."

"Oh, you think so?" A panty-melting smile swept across his face as he said, "I'll be sure to keep that in mind."

We continued talking as we ate our sandwiches, and when we were done, Wyatt put our dishes in the sink and asked, "You ready for that movie?"

"Sure."

I followed him into the living room and over to the sofa. As soon as we were seated, he grabbed one of his blankets and draped it over us. He grabbed the remote and started flipping through the channels. "Action? Comedy? What are you in the mood for?"

"Anything is fine with me." When he stopped on one of the old Rambo movies, I shook my head and said, "Except that."

"Why? You got something against Rambo?"

"No, I'm just not in the mood for a trigger-happy militant with a bad haircut." His mouth dropped like he was wounded by my comment, so I asked, "Why? Is this your favorite movie or something?"

"No, I wouldn't say that, but Rambo is one of the classics."

"A classic? I think you're pushing it there a little."

"No way." Wyatt's brows furrowed. "He's a Vietnam War veteran who takes justice into his own hands. The man is an American legend."

"Who made his name by blowing people up."

"*He's a highly skilled soldier.*"

"Um-hmm."

"You know, it's not just about blowing people up. There's an emotional side, too."

"Oh really?"

"Absolutely. He's struggling to process his own trauma from the war. The whole thing speaks to the strength of humanity in the face of adversity."

I started giggling as I said, "I can't tell if you are being serious right now."

"Of course, I'm being serious." His face showed zero emotion as he told me,

"You can't go wrong when you're fighting for what's right."

"Okay, fine. We can watch it."

"Nah." A lopsided grin crept across his face. "I'm not in the mood for an American legend tonight."

"Seriously?" I gave him a nudge and chuckled, "You put me through all that for nothing."

"Just giving you some insight on a classic." He started flipping through the channels, and when he couldn't find something that appealed to him, he offered the remote to me. "Your turn."

"Okay, but I don't think I'm going to have any better luck." I started flipping through the various movie channels, and it wasn't long before I came across an old Morgan Freeman movie. "How about this one?"

"Looks good to me."

We both settled in on the sofa, and it wasn't long before we were both engrossed in the movie. It was a thriller where several women were being held captive in a cave—one of them being Freeman's niece. It was an older movie, but Wyatt seemed to be enjoying it. I didn't really care about the movie. I was just happy to be there with him.

When it was over, I motioned my hand towards the screen and announced, "I knew it was him."

"Oh, really?"

"Yep." I rested my head on Wyatt's shoulder. "They always try and make it the guy you least expect, but they're the ones I always expect the most."

"So, you knew that from the start that it was the cop?"

"No, but all that good ol' boy, 'I'll take care of you and watch over you' stuff, is always a red flag. They try to give you this false sense of security by making the bad guy look innocent. It never works, especially when it's some sweet, little old guy who lives alone and has no life." I was tired and rambling when I closed my eyes and told him, "They are always the ones with some shady background that no one thought to check out."

"You're right."

Wyatt sat up, and I could tell by his expression that something was wrong, but I had no idea what had him so rattled. After several seconds, he stood and said, "I've gotta go."

"What? Right now?" I glanced over at the clock as I told him, "It's after midnight."

"I know." He rushed down the hall towards his room as he explained, "There's something I need to look into."

"Now?" I got up from the sofa and followed him down the hall as I asked, "Is something wrong?"

"I can't get into it."

"So, it has something to do with the club?"

When he didn't respond, I knew I had my answer.

I knew better than to ask any more questions.

Club business was never discussed with anyone other than the brothers, so I left it alone and started changing back into my clothes. I'd just put back on my jeans and was about to take off Wyatt's t-shirt when he said, "Keep it."

He stepped over to me and lowered his mouth to mine. The second our lips connected, my entire body came alive. Needing more, I lifted my hand up to his face, urging him closer as his tongue delved deeper into my mouth. The bristles of his beard were rough against my palm, but his lips were soft and warm, luring me in for more. His touch was tender and sweet, sending a wave of heat rushing over me. I was just about to get swept away when he withdrew his mouth and rested his forehead to mine. "I've gotta go."

Doing my best to hide my disappointment, I nodded and finished gathering my things. A blink later, we were out the door, and my date with Wyatt was over. Damn. That was not how I thought it would play out, but things rarely ever go the way I think they will.

CHAPTER 10
Bones

I hated to cut our date short, especially after such an amazing night, but I didn't have a choice. Elsie's comments about the movie started me thinking about the unknown still out there lurking in the shadows. I knew in my gut there was something or someone waiting to be found, and my mind wouldn't rest until I found it.

When we got to the clubhouse, I walked Elsie down to her room, and after one last kiss goodnight, I made my way to the computer room. I grabbed the files in question and got to work. I started with Jack Bivens, the owner of the first camera we'd found. Big and Cotton both knew Jack. Hell, everyone in town knew him. He was a retired pharmacist and owned just over six acres of property, all monitored through security cameras.

I ran a full background check on Jack, checking for anything that might be considered a red flag. Big and I had already been through all this before. We'd dotted all the i's and crossed all the t's, but this time, I wasn't letting a personal connection to the club or community deter me from digging deeper.

I checked his full history, along with each member of his family, but found nothing. So, I moved on to Porter Davis, an industrial electrician who lived in a small cabin out by Olympic Park. He didn't have much land or anything else for that matter, but his name was in the file.

One hour had rolled into the next and I was beyond exhausted, but I kept at it. I was determined to find something—anything. I was so lost in my research that I didn't even notice that Big had walked in. He stepped over to my desk and peered over my shoulder as he asked, "What's all this?"

"I'm just looking into a few things."

"Jack Bivens?" Big picked up his file and sifted through it. "Why are you looking into him?"

"I'm looking into them all." I ran my hand over my face, trying to wake myself up. "I think you were onto something with the cameras, so I'm double-checking a few things."

"But we all know Jack. He and his family have

been here since I was a kid." Big's eyes narrowed. "Why would you waste your time with him?"

"'Cause it's always the ones with some shady background that no one thought to check out."

"What the fuck are you talking about, brother?"

"We gotta just assume that everyone is guilty... including the people we've known for years."

"So, what exactly are you looking for?"

"I'm not sure." I leaned back in my chair as I told him, "Maybe one of them has spent some time in the pen or has a tie to the military."

"O-*kay*." He sat down at the table across from me, then studied me for a moment. "How long have you been at this?"

"Since about midnight."

"That's what I figured. You need to get your ass up and go get in the fucking bed."

"But..."

"But nothing," he scolded. "You're no good to anyone like this. Get some sleep, and we'll pick this back up in a few hours."

I didn't bother arguing. I knew he was right, so I got up and headed down to my room. My head barely touched my pillow before I was out, and I was out for hours. I probably would've slept for hours longer if I hadn't heard Rooster shout, "I told you that seal wasn't gonna work! Now, I'm gonna have to replace the whole damn manifold."

"It would've worked if you hadn't been in such a fucking rush!" Torch roared back. "You didn't give the epoxy time to set."

"Nobody's got that kind of time."

"It's gonna take a hell of a lot longer to replace the manifold than it would've taken that epoxy to set."

I was tempted to shout curses at them and tell them to shut the fuck up, but I just lay there and listened as they made their way down the hall. I waited until I heard them go out the back door, then I got up and went to the bathroom. I brushed my teeth and threw some cold water on my face; then I headed back down to the work room. When I walked in, I expected to find Big working at his desk, but he was nowhere to be found.

I walked over to the desk, and everything was exactly the way I'd left it. Big hadn't added anything to it. As far as I could tell, he hadn't even looked at the files I'd put together—which meant he thought it was all a waste of time. While that stung, it wasn't enough to keep me from continuing on with my investigation.

I took out Big's original file and went down to the next name. I did a complete scan of Daniel Marquis and everyone he was connected to, then moved on to the next name and the next. I spent hours upon hours searching for something that might be worth mentioning to Big or Cotton, but sadly, I found nothing.

It was late and I was starting to feel the effects of my exhaustion, but I wasn't ready to give up. I located the next name and was about to dive in when there was a tap at the door. When I looked up, I found my mother's worried eyes staring back at me. "Hey, stranger. How's it going?"

"It's going." I eased back from my desk as I asked, "What are you doing here?"

"Griffin had something to take care of, so I came with him. Thought it'd give me a chance to come by and check in with you." She stepped into the room as she told me, "I know you think I'm silly, but I haven't seen you in a few days and wanted to make sure you're okay."

"I'm fine. Just been busy."

"I can see that." She gave me one of her mothering looks. "Looks like you've been at this for a while."

"I have been, and I'm gonna be at it for a while longer."

"Well, can I get you something? A drink or a bite to eat?"

"Thanks, but I'm good." I didn't want her to worry, so I told her, "I'm gonna work another hour, and then, I'm gonna call it a night."

"Okay, then I won't keep you." She walked over and gave me a tight hug, then kissed me on the forehead as she said, "I miss you, kiddo. I need to spend some time with you soon, okay?"

I nodded, then promised, "Soon."

She studied me for a moment, then turned and started out of the room. "I'm gonna hold you to that."

"I know you will."

I couldn't help but smile as I watched her close the door behind her. I was a grown man, fully capable of taking care of myself, but my wonderful mother would always be my mother. It was in her nature to take care of the people she loved. I felt a little guilty that I hadn't told her about Elsie. It wasn't that I didn't want her to know.

I did.

But with everything that was going on, I didn't have the time or the patience to answer a million questions. So, I would wait and tell her all about it when things settled down. I just had to make sure I told her before someone else beat me to it.

I worked for another hour, then decided to call it a night and headed back to my room. I was tempted to stop by and check in with Elsie, but it was already after one. I figured she was already in bed, so I pulled out my phone and sent her a quick text.

. . .

Me:

> Hey. Sorry I've been MIA.
> It was a long night and even longer day.
> Hope you had a good one.

Once I was done, I continued down to my room and straight into the bathroom. I took a long, hot shower and put on some clean boxers, then crashed into bed. I hadn't been lying there long when my phone chimed with a message. I quickly grabbed it from the side table and smiled when I looked down at the screen.

Elsie:

> Hey-
> Sorry to hear you had such a long day.
> I hope everything's okay.

Me:

> I figured you'd be asleep.

Elsie:

> I'm a little restless tonight.

. . .

Me:

Come down to my room.

Elsie:

That's okay. I'll be fine.

Me:

Elsie

Elsie:

Wyatt

I'd always loved that she'd never called me by my road name. It was either Wyatt or nothing. Chuckling under my breath, I sent her one final message.

Me:

My room.
Now.

. . .

I returned my phone to the bedside table, and it wasn't long before my door crept open, and light flooded into the dark room. Elsie stepped into the room, then closed the door behind her. "Hey."

"Hey." I lifted the covers and that's all it took for her to crawl in next to me. I slipped my arm around her waist and pulled her close, and within a breath, my entire body started to relax. "That's better."

"Yes, it is."

"You have a long day, too?"

"You could say that."

"Something happen?"

"No, I just got in my head a little, and once the wheels get to turning, it's hard to shut them off."

"So, you had something on your mind."

She nodded, then sighed. "Today would've been Brantley's twenty-first birthday."

"Oh, damn. I had no idea."

"I know you didn't. It's fine." Her voice trembled as she told me, "I went out to the cemetery for a while. I thought it would make me feel closer to him or whatever, but it only made me miss him more. My parents, too. I know it's been a long time and I should be over it by now... but I don't think I'll ever stop missing them."

"I'm sorry. I wish I could do something to make it better."

"You already have." She glanced up at me with a

half-smile. "You've always been there when I needed you most."

"And I always will be."

Elsie didn't respond. She simply rested her head on my chest and closed her eyes, and it wasn't long before her body grew limp and her breaths shallow. I was beginning to think she'd drifted off to sleep until I heard her whisper, "Thank you, Wyatt. Thank you for everything."

Without saying anything more, she drifted off to sleep, and with the sounds of her soft, soothing breaths, it didn't take long for me to follow after. The next morning, I woke up with Elsie sprawled across my bed, and she looked absolutely beautiful. She was wearing a pair of pink knit shorts and a long sleeve t-shirt, and her lips were full and pouty from sleeping hard.

I wanted nothing more than to kiss her and fuck her long and hard, but she was sleeping so soundly, I hated to wake her. Besides, I had work that needed to be done, so I eased out of bed and got dressed. I left Elsie a note, then made my way to the kitchen for some coffee and a bite to eat. It was still early. The sun was just starting to rise, so I was able to make my coffee and go without the hassle of talking to anyone.

When I got to my desk, I took out the list of names that we'd compiled, and I studied it for several moments, and for reasons I still don't understand, my eyes fell on the name David Bruton. I passed by it several times, but I kept coming back to it. I don't know why I became so fixated on it.

Bruton was a name I'd heard many times.

He was a retired history teacher in his late fifties. He was widowed with two sons who both lived in the city, but he busied himself with the town council and church every Sunday. He owned various properties throughout town, along with two large warehouses down at the dock—each with their own motion-censored security camera.

They monitored both the property and the road.

I had no reason not to believe that Bruton was an all-around good guy, but I followed my instincts and started digging into his history. I started with the basics. His address, his phone number, and his social. Everything panned out, so I moved on to his work history. Everything looked legit until the summer of '98.

There was nothing before that.

No job. No address. No phone number. Nothing.

The trail had run dry, so I did the only thing I could. I found an old picture of him and ran it through BioID—our facial recognition software. The first scan came up with nothing, so I searched online for a different image. I sent it through, and after a lengthy search, the name Carl Davenport appeared on the screen.

I knew right then that I had found something big—something that made my hours and hours of research worthwhile. I typed his name into the search engine, and within seconds, a long list of Carl Davenports popped up on the screen. I started going through each of them until I spotted a photograph that looked similar to the original image I had for Bruton. A few more clicks, and then, I saw the logo for Interpol.

I froze.

I simply couldn't believe what I was seeing.

Interpol is an international policing agency.

They tracked down the most wanted criminals and have connections all over the world. My original theory was beginning to make sense, and then again, it wasn't. I couldn't fathom how David Bruton, the high school history teacher, was actually Carl Davenport, an Interpol investigator. I stared at the screen a moment longer, making sure I had it right, then stood and rushed to the door.

I opened it and stuck my head out into the hall. When I spotted Maverick, I shouted, "Yo, Mav!"

"Yeah?"

"I need you to find Big. Tell him to get his ass down here now!"

"Why? What's going on?"

"I found him!"

"Found who?"

"Bruton!" He gave me a puzzled look, and I knew he had no idea what I was talking about. I didn't have time to explain, so I shouted, "Get Big!"

He nodded, then disappeared down the hall.

I went back over to my desk and started looking back over everything I'd found. I had no idea how Bruton would've gone from working for an international policing agency to teaching history at our local high school. It seemed farfetched, and I was beginning to think that I had it all wrong—until my personal cell phone chimed with a message.

I took it out of my pocket, and I was shaken to the core when I read:

Unknown Caller:
I was wondering when you'd finally find me.

CHAPTER 11
Elsie

After a long, emotional day, I'd fallen asleep in Wyatt's arms, and I'd slept better than I had in weeks. So well, in fact, that I'd overslept and was running late for class. I had to jump out of bed and rush down the hall to take a shower. I didn't even have time to be bothered that I'd woken up in bed alone.

As soon as I was dressed, I headed out to the parking lot. I opened my door and had just thrown my bag into the backseat when I heard Cotton ask, "Where are you running off to so early this morning?"

"I've got class," I answered with a yawn. "I'm going in a little early, so I can catch up on my notes."

Cotton nodded, then asked, "So, are things going good with school?"

"Yeah, they're going great." I wouldn't have even

had the opportunity to go to college if it hadn't been for Cotton and the brothers. They'd not only helped pay for my classes, but they had supported me and encouraged me every step of the way. "I'm hoping to get my information on graduation by next week."

"Good deal." A smile crossed his face as he said, "Proud of you, Else."

"Thank you, Cotton." I stepped over and gave him a quick hug. "I couldn't have done it without you."

"I don't know about that." He chuckled. "You're a stubborn one. You'd find a way—with or without us."

"Maybe, but you gotta know that I'll always be grateful for you and the brothers."

"I do." He motioned his hand towards my car. "Now, go on. Get to class."

I nodded, then got in my car and headed to campus. It was cold, murky, and looked like snow, but I didn't mind. I was in a great mood, and I wasn't going to let anything bring me down. When I got to the communications building, I was pleased to see that there was a parking place right up front. I quickly nabbed it, then grabbed my bag and started inside.

I hadn't gotten far when I heard someone call out my name.

"Elsie!" I turned, and my stomach sank when I spotted Ben rushing over to me. "Hey, how's it going?"

"Hey, Ben. It's going okay." He seemed different

today, and it wasn't just the fact that he'd traded his typical dress shirt and khakis for a black hoodie and jeans. He seemed agitated and off-center. It was unsettling. Not that it mattered. I had no interest in sharing a lengthy conversation with him, so I said, "I was just about to head into class."

"I thought that class didn't start until ten."

I was a little thrown that he knew when my class started, but I let it go. "It does. I was just going to do a little studying beforehand."

"Oh, okay."

"Was there something you needed?"

"Yeah, uh..." He lowered his head and nervously toyed with a rock. "I just um... I just wanted to apologize for the other night."

"Oh, that's not necessary."

"But it is." He actually sounded sincere as he told me, "I don't know what was up with me that night, but I shouldn't have said all that stuff about your friends."

"No, you shouldn't have, but I appreciate you apologizing."

"It's the least I could do, especially after I made such a mess of our date."

"It's fine. Everything worked out."

"I don't know if I'd say that." He grimaced as he said, "You left me high and dry at the restaurant. It wasn't exactly the way I'd hoped the night would go."

"Me either, but maybe it was for the best." I glanced down at my watch, then said, "I'm sorry, but I really should get going."

"Okay." When I turned to leave, he quickly asked, "Hey, you wanna grab some coffee after class? Maybe do a quick review for the big Spanish test this afternoon."

"Spanish test?" My heart sank at the thought. "Oh my God. I can't believe I forgot about that."

"It's supposed to be a real kick in the ass, but we can cram and get you ready."

After my weekend with Wyatt, it didn't feel right to make plans to meet up with another man, especially Ben, but I was in a bind. I had to pass that test, so I told him, "That would be great."

"Awesome. I'll um..." He appeared to become anxious once again but quickly shook it off and said, "I'll meet you at the coffee shop when class is over."

"Okay. Sounds good."

"I'll see you then."

I nodded, then turned and headed inside to class. As I'd hoped, I got there before class started and had time to go over my notes from the previous week. Eventually, the teacher came in, and class started. I tried to pay attention, but my mind kept drifting to

Wyatt and the weekend we'd shared. Wyatt was not only attentive and sweet, but he was funny, and I found it endearing when he opened up to me about Stitch and the brothers.

I couldn't remember a time when I'd enjoyed myself more. It was a thought that had me second-guessing my decision to meet up with Ben. It was just to go over Spanish. Nothing more. He was smart and attractive, but I had no real interest in him. I never did —at least, nothing like I had for Wyatt. I'd known that all along, and now, it was time that he knew it, too.

When class was over, I gathered my things and headed over to the coffee shop. As promised, Ben was waiting for me there. He was sitting at one of the back tables with two cups of coffee and a smile. I felt a cringe creep over me as I made my way over to him and said, "Um, I'm sorry, but I don't think our cram session is a good idea."

"Why not?"

"I've got some errands I need to run."

"I could take you."

"No, that's not necessary."

"It's not a problem," he pushed. "I've got time to kill."

He wasn't getting the hint, or he just didn't care. Either way, I was about to make myself clear. "Thanks, but *I'm going to go alone.*"

"What about the test?"

"I'll figure it out." Before I could say anything more, my phone started to ring. I took it out of my purse, and when I looked down at the screen, I was surprised to see that it was Cassidy calling. "Hello?"

"Hey, Else. It's Cass." She sounded concerned as she asked, "Are you still at school?"

"Yeah, I just got out of class."

"Does that mean you're planning to head back soon?"

"Not exactly." I didn't want Ben to overhear my conversation, so I gave a quick wave goodbye and started for the door. "I have a test at one. Why? Is something wrong?"

"Cotton has called for a lockdown."

"Oh."

I'd lived at the clubhouse long enough to know that a lockdown meant the brothers were concerned about the safety of the brothers and their families. They'd bring them all into the clubhouse, and they'd do everything in their power to keep everyone safe.

The guys would try and act like it wasn't a big deal, but I knew better. I could see the mix of worry and fight in their eyes, and I had my suspicions about what had put it there—which made me wonder if someone had gotten hurt. "Did something happen? Is everyone okay?"

"No, everyone's fine. Cotton's just taking precautions."

"Okay. Understood... Do I need to come back now?"

"No, no. You don't have to do that. Just send me the address of where you'll be, and I'll tell Cotton to have one of the guys come and keep an eye on you."

"Okay." I got in my car and closed the door, then quickly sent her the address. "Are you sure everything's okay?"

"Everything's fine. Nothing for you to worry about."

"Okay.... Well, I'll see you in a couple of hours then."

"Sounds good. You be careful."

"I will."

I ended the call, then tossed my phone over to the seat next to me. I started my car and was about to back out when I spotted Ben standing at the front of my car. He had a vicious look on his face—one that sent a cold chill down my spine, and I had no idea why. I'd tried to be considerate of his feelings, but clearly, he wasn't pleased that I'd decided not to stay and study with him. I was torn. I didn't know if I should apologize or just get the hell out of there.

Something in my gut told me to just leave, so that's exactly what I did. I whipped out of that parking place and drove over to the student union. I figured it would be a safe place to grab a bite to eat and study. I found a parking spot between it and the Keller building where I'd be taking my Spanish test. After I'd parked, I took a quick look around, checking for anything or anyone that might seem suspicious, and once I saw that everything was okay, I headed inside.

It was lunchtime, so the place was brimming with students. I usually didn't like it when it was this crowded, but today, it made me feel safer. I grabbed a slice of pizza and a soda, then found a quiet spot in the back corner by the window. I opened my Spanish notes and started studying while I ate.

I hadn't been studying long when I heard Torch say, "Hey, Squirt. How's it going?"

"Fine. Just getting a little studying in." I couldn't help but notice that all eyes were on Torch and Wrath as they sat down across from me. I couldn't blame my classmates for staring. Torch and Wrath looked a little out of place with their tattoos and black leather jackets. "So, um, Cotton sent you?"

"Just as a precaution," Wrath answered.

"Cass said the same thing." I found it doubtful that either of them would tell me much, but I hoped they would answer, "Is everyone okay? Is Wyatt okay?"

"Yeah, he's fine. He'd be here if he could, but he's ah... working on something."

"I'm just glad everyone's okay."

Torch looked around the room, and a mischievous smirk inched across his lips when he spotted a table full of girls. "What is it about college girls that makes them so fucking hot?"

"You do realize that I'm a college girl?"

"Yeah, but you don't count. You're Elsie. You're Bones' girl."

"It's funny how everyone seemed to know that but me."

"Poor kid has been hung up on you since day one. Got no idea how you didn't see it."

"I'm pretty sure I was the one who was hung up on him, but that's neither here nor there."

I wasn't quite ready for my test, so I didn't say anything more and got back to looking over my notes. The guys did their best to remain quiet and let me study, but sadly, it wasn't long before Torch leaned over and whispered, "You're gonna have to bring some of these chicks to the next club party."

"I hate to break it to you, but I don't even know these girls. And the girls I do know would probably run scared at the sight of you two."

"Whoa." Torch's brows furrowed. "That hurts. That hurts deep."

"Sorry, but it's true. Now, let me study, or I'm gonna bomb this test."

Like a pouting child, Torch let out a frustrated breath, then leaned back in his chair. For the next half hour, he and Wrath remained silent and let me finish preparing for my test. When I was done, they followed me over to the Keller building. They were about to walk inside with me until I said, "You guys can just wait for me here. I won't be long."

"Straight in, straight out?" Wrath asked.

"Yeah. I promise."

He nodded, then watched intently as I turned and started inside. I was just about to open the door when I spotted Ben in my peripheral. He was just standing there, watching me, and when he realized I'd seen him, he bolted. I figured he'd just gone around to the other entrance, but when I got to the classroom, there was no sign of him.

I thought it was strange that he was skipping the test, but honestly, I had too many other things on my mind to care what Ben did or didn't do. I took my stupid test, and when I was done, I felt pretty good about it. I met back up with the guys, and they followed me to the clubhouse. By the time we got back, the place was a madhouse.

All the brothers were busy helping their ol' ladies and kids get everything moved into their rooms, and it was utter chaos. I felt like I was in the way, so I made myself scarce and went to my room. I checked my phone to see if I had any missed messages, but sadly, I had none. I could've used the time to get a little studying in, but I wasn't in the mood and opted for a movie instead.

I crawled into bed and turned on my TV. It took a little searching, but I eventually found a romantic comedy with Patrick Dempsey. I grabbed a cold coffee from my mini fridge, then curled back up on my bed. It wasn't long before I was caught up in the push and pull of the main characters. While it was different, there were aspects of the movie that reminded me of my relationship with Wyatt.

The main characters were best friends, and the heroine was crazy about him— only neither of them knew it. She had to meet someone else and almost marry him before either of them came to their senses. Thankfully, it just took a silly date with Ben to draw Wyatt's attention, and since then, things couldn't have been better.

He was loving and attentive, and over the past few days, our friendship had only grown stronger. It was a thought that had me wishing he was there watching the movie with me. Curious to see if things had died down, I got up, and when I peeked out in the hall, I was pleased to see that things were finally settling down. I was just about to close the door when I heard Wyatt say, "Hey."

"Hey." I opened the door wider and watched as he stepped inside my room. Just looking at him made it hard to breathe, hard to think, and I could tell by the look in his eyes that he felt the same when he looked at me. "I wasn't expecting to see you. I figured you'd be busy with the brothers."

"I can't stay. I just wanted to come and make sure you made it back."

"Yeah, Torch and Wrath came and kept an eye on things while I was in class."

"Good." He stepped closer. "I would've come myself, but I was working on something. I still am. That's why I have to get back."

"That's okay. I understand."

He stood there just staring at me; the onslaught of emotions raging in his eyes stole my breath. My heart skipped a beat when he brought his hand up to my throat and gently wrapped his fingers around my neck. He guided me forward as he leaned over and pressed his mouth to mine, kissing me tenderly, *possessively*.

In that moment, it was just him and me, and it was the most incredible feeling I'd ever experienced. His hands dropped to my waist, and a small, needful moan vibrated through my chest as he pulled me closer. The caress of his lips was magic, making me feel like I was floating on air.

He deepened the kiss, but only for a moment.

Time wasn't on our side, so I wasn't surprised when he took a step back, breaking free from our embrace. We both stood there gazing at one another. Neither of us said a word. We knew exactly what that kiss meant.

The feelings we'd been experiencing were mutual, and as much as we wanted to act on them, they would have to wait—at least for now. Wyatt rested his forehead on mine as he whispered, "I have to go."

"I know."

"I'll be back when I can."

"I hope that's sooner than later."

"You and me both."

He gave me one last kiss, then turned and left the room, leaving me alone once again. Still feeling the sensation of having his mouth on mine, I brought my hand up to my face and ran my fingers across my lips. I missed it. I missed him and wondered when I might actually get to see him again.

I couldn't be sure, but I had a nagging feeling that it was going to be longer than any of us cared to imagine.

CHAPTER 12
Bones

Patience had never been one of my strong suits, especially when my brothers' lives were at stake. I'd tried to hold out and wait for Big to come to me, but time was of the essence. I had to tell him what I'd found, so I left the office and went to track them down. When Rooster told me he was in Cotton's office with Stitch, I headed straight there. I knocked on the door, and without giving anyone a chance to answer, I charged inside. Big, Stitch, and Cotton all turned and looked at me like I'd lost my mind, so I wasted no time saying, "I found a lead on who's been fucking with the club."

"What?" Cotton's back stiffened. "How'd you manage that?"

"I've been looking into the camera thing," I

answered. "I picked up where Big and I left off, and I..."

Before I could finish my thought, Stitch turned to Big and said, "You said the camera thing was a dead end."

"I did, but maybe I was wrong."

"David Bruton."

"Yeah?" Cotton sounded intrigued. "What about him?"

"He's our guy."

"You talking about the history teacher?"

"Yeah, that's him, but he's not who you think he is."

I told them about the movie Elsie and I had watched and how it had gotten me to think that the men we were after might be right here under our noses. I told them how I'd started going through each of the names on Big's list and how the first few background checks came up clear. None of them said a word as I told them about Bruton's work history and how it ended in '98. "The trail ran dry, so I used our facial recognition software. That's when I found that his name is actually Carl Davenport, and he used to work for Interpol."

"Interpol?" Cotton leaned back in his chair with a scowl. "Seriously?"

"He was with them for twelve years. That would've

given him plenty of time to make connections with some pretty shady folks."

"I had no idea."

"No one did. That's the point."

"Yeah, but this is Mr. Bruton we're talking about." Big sounded skeptical as he told him, "He's like seventy-something, and he's lived here for as long as I can remember. Hell, he's on the town council. I find it hard to believe that he's our guy."

"Yeah, I thought the same until I got this."

I took my phone out of my pocket and showed them the message I'd received. Cotton sounded pissed when he roared, "What the fuck?"

"How the hell did he know you found him?"

"I have no idea."

"You didn't say anything to anyone else?"

"No. I came straight here." I looked at Big as I said, "We secured the server, so I know he wasn't watching me there. Maybe he had his name flagged or something."

"Possibly, but how did he know it was you?"

"Oh, shit. *Wait...* I forgot. I saw Maverick." With everything that had happened, I'd totally forgotten that I'd spoken to him. "I told him that I'd found something on Bruton and for him to go find you."

"Where was this?"

"Right outside my door."

Stitch sounded distressed when he asked Big, "When was the last time you two did a sweep of the club?"

"Not since the New Year's gathering, but nobody's been here. Just us. There's no way anyone could've planted something without us knowing it."

We had all the necessary devices to check the clubhouse for bugs and hidden cameras, and even though we'd used them frequently, we'd never actually found anything. I wasn't surprised. There were always two or more brothers at the gate, guarding against any intruders, and we had cameras that we monitored on a daily basis, especially when we had outsiders on the grounds.

"Where there's a will, there's a way."

I could feel the tension radiating off of Stitch as I offered, "We could do a sweep now and see if we can find anything."

"No. We'll take care of it." Cotton replied. "Right now, I need you and Big to find everything you can on Davenport. I want to know what kind of business he's in and who he has on the payroll."

"We'll see what we can find out," Big answered.

Cotton turned back to me as he said, "And if he reaches out to you again, I want to be the first to know about it."

"You got it."

Without saying anything more, Big and I turned

and walked out of Cotton's office. We'd just started down the hall when Big asked, "You got any idea how he got your number?"

"No clue."

"Damn." Big shook his head. "David Bruton. I never would've thought it."

"I'd say that's what he's countin' on." My mind was still clouded with doubt, so I added, "I'm not positive that he's the one behind all this, but the pieces seem to fit."

"Then, let's see what else we can find on him and see where we stand."

As soon as we got back to the office, I showed Big everything I'd found, and he agreed that Bruton's past definitely looked suspicious. "We need to find everything we can on his time at Interpol. From what cases he was working on to who he was working with. We also need to know if he made any arrests or if he'd made any contacts."

"Their security is going to be intense. Hacking into their database isn't going to be easy."

"We can do it." Big started up his laptop. "It's just going to take some time and a little fancy footwork."

I nodded, then we both got to work on breaking into Interpol. As I feared, it was heavily secured, but thankfully, it wasn't anything that Big and I couldn't handle. After a couple of hours, we'd made our way in and were searching for everything we could find on Carl Davenport. I was just as eager as Big to find out what was going on with the guy, but I'd been at this thing for days.

I was struggling to keep my focus, and I couldn't stop thinking about Elsie and our last kiss. Thinking a quick visit with her would ease my mind and get me back on track, I stood and said, "I've got something I need to take care of. I'll be right back."

Without giving him a chance to respond, I walked out of the room and headed down to Elsie's room. When I walked up, she was looking out into the hall, more than likely checking to see if things had finally settled down, and when she spotted me, a smile swept over her beautiful face. Damn. Just one look at her, and I was itching to touch her. Hold her. Kiss her.

Unable to resist, I stepped into her room, pulled her close, and pressed my lips against hers. I could feel the beating of her heart against my chest as she inched closer. She moaned against my lips as I delved deeper into her mouth, relishing in her taste, her warmth.

Absolute perfection.

There was no denying it. I was lost in her touch, like a man under a spell, and for a brief moment, everything around us stilled. The moment didn't last long, but it gave me a much-needed reprieve. When I got back to the workroom, I sat down at my desk, and I was about to get to work when Big asked, "She okay?"

"Yeah, she's good."

Big knew me well, so I wasn't surprised that he knew I'd gone to see Elsie. But Big being Big, he didn't give me hell about it. He understood how I felt and left it alone. We both got back to work, and it wasn't long before we started to compile an intriguing file of information—like the fact that he'd worked on a hundred or more cases but only made a handful of arrests.

I felt like we were on the right track when the workroom door flew open, and Stitch and Cotton stormed into the room. "Sorry, guys, but you're gonna have to stop what you're doing and pull up the camera feed."

"Why?" Big asked. "What's going on?"

"This is what's going on."

Stitch opened his hand, and the second Big saw the small camera resting in the center of his palm, he growled, "What the hell? Did you find that here?"

"Afraid so."

"Where the hell was it?"

"At the front entrance," Cotton answered. "We need to check the cameras and see if we can figure out who planted it."

"That's gonna take some time." Big turned back to

his computer and pulled up the security. "Any idea where we should start?"

"I figure we need to go back to New Year's." Stitch stepped closer as he said, "Need to see anyone and everyone who's come in or out of that door."

"That's a high-traffic area, brother."

"I'm aware, but it's gotta be done."

Big nodded, then started going through the feed. It was a slow process. There were hours on end of the footage, and it didn't help matters that there was so much movement in that particular area. There was no missing the frustration in Stitch's voice when he growled, "This is taking too fucking long."

"Maybe there's a faster way."

"Whatcha got in mind?"

I stood and walked over to them as I said, "We don't need to look through every second of footage. We just need to focus on times when outsiders are around, especially when they hit that front door."

"Yeah, but we've already talked about this. We haven't had any outsiders since New Year's."

"Do we know that for certain? Cause I have my doubts about it." He shook his head as he grumbled, "Hell, we all know Rooster and the boys bring chicks over here all the time."

"We won't know until we know."

We started going back through all the footage, only

slowing down when we noticed anything unusual, but it was slow and aggravating. The tension in the room was growing by the second, and we were all about to reach our limits when I spotted Elsie in that damn mini-skirt and a long, cable-knit sweater. It was the outfit she'd worn on the night of her date.

I could still remember how pissed I was about the thing. I didn't want her to go out with him. Hell, just the thought of it had me spiraling, but I couldn't say shit about it. I hadn't claimed her, and like it or not, she was free to see whomever she wanted. I watched as she made her way down the hall, and not long after, Rooster and I gave her and her date a hard time.

Rooster was reaming the guy pretty hard, and Elsie, too. They both looked pretty rattled. I almost felt bad for them, and then I noticed that he had his hand behind his back. I stepped closer as I told Big, "Go back a bit."

"Why? Did you see something?"

"Yeah." I pointed to the screen as I said, "Check out the guy's hands. Is it just me, or is he up to something?"

"It definitely looks suspicious." Big zoomed in, giving us all a better view of his hands, and there was no doubt that he'd stuck something on the wall. "I think we found our guy."

"So, who is he?"

"Pretty sure he goes to school with her."

"We're gonna need more than that." Cotton walked over and opened the door, then called out, "Yo, Torch. Go get Elsie. We need a word with her."

As soon as he closed the door, Stitch turned to me and asked, "You gonna be good with staying for this or …"

"I'm not going anywhere."

"Understood."

We all knew Elsie had done nothing wrong. She'd just gone out on a date with the wrong fucking guy. But there were questions that had to be asked. Thankfully, I trusted my brothers to ask them in a way that wouldn't scare Elsie or make her feel like she had wronged us in some way.

We hadn't been waiting long when Torch opened the door and guided Elsie inside. She'd changed into a pair of sweats with the t-shirt I'd given her, and it got me right in the gut. Her eyes were wide with worry as she looked around the room and listened anxiously as Torch asked, "Need anything else?"

"No, we're good."

Torch nodded, then made his way out of the room. As soon as he was gone, Elsie turned to me and said, "Hey, guys. What's going on?"

"We need to talk to you about something."

"Okay. What about?"

Stitch kept his voice low and steady as he told her, "The guy you went out with... The one who came here to pick you up."

"Ben? Why do you need to know about him?"

"It's important, Else." I stepped over to her. "We wouldn't ask if it wasn't."

"I don't know what to tell you. Um... His name is Ben Bruton."

"Bruton?"

"Yeah, I believe David Bruton is his grandfather." Cotton turned to Stitch and cocked his brow. When Elsie saw his reaction, she added, "But I might be wrong about that. He never really mentioned him."

"How'd the two of you meet?"

"At school." Her eyes remained locked on mine as she said, "We have a few classes together. He seemed like a nice guy, so when he asked me out, I said yes."

"You don't know where he's from or anything about his family?"

"I assumed he lives close, and he never really said much about his family, just that he had a sister. It sounded like they were pretty close." Her face was marked with worry as she said, "We only went out twice, so there's not much more to tell."

"Did he ever ask about us?"

"Hmm, he was pretty curious about how I ended up living here. He also asked what you were into." She glanced over at Stitch. "He wanted to know if you were running guns or selling drugs. That's when I decided to end the date."

I didn't like this.

It was too much.

Every muscle in my body had grown tense, and my head had started to pound. I was quickly approaching my brink, so I clenched my fists at my sides and dug my nails into my palms. I took several deep breaths and tried to focus on the sound of the ceiling fan above me, hoping it would be enough to settle me.

It didn't.

Hell, I was so worked up that I almost didn't hear my phone when it chimed with a new text message. At first, I ignored it and kept my focus on Elsie, but when it chimed a second time, I grabbed it from my pocket and muted the ringer. I was about to put it back in my pocket when I happened to notice that I'd received another message. My blood ran cold when I read:

Unknown Caller:
CHECK YOUR EMAIL

CHAPTER 13
Elsie

I had no idea why Cotton and the others were so interested in Ben, but it clearly wasn't good. I could literally feel the rage radiating off of them, and I couldn't understand why. I wasn't interested in him, but he seemed like a decent enough guy. He certainly didn't seem like the type to get on the Satan's Fury radar. I was tempted to ask why they were so interested in him, but I knew better. They were already on edge, and I had no interest in rousing them any further.

"What did you tell him?"

"I said rumors were just rumors, and this was one that didn't deem repeating. After that, I got up and left."

"Have you seen or talked to him since?"

"Actually, I saw him today." My eyes skirted over to

Wyatt as I added, "I was about to go into class when he came over to me and apologized for the things he'd said."

"And that was it?"

"Pretty much." I shrugged. "He reminded me about a Spanish test we were having today and offered to meet up with me at the coffee shop to study."

"Did you go?"

"Yes, but I didn't stay." I glanced over at Wyatt, checking to see if he looked upset, but he was looking at his phone and didn't even seem to be listening to me. "I just went there to tell him that I had some things I had to take care of and would just study on my own."

"Did he seem bothered that you weren't staying?"

"I don't think he was all that happy about it, but I didn't really give him a chance to say anything. When Cass called to tell me about the lockdown, I walked out."

I glanced back over at Wyatt, checking once again to see if he seemed bothered, but like before, he wasn't paying the least bit of attention to my conversation with Cotton and Stitch. Instead, he was over in the corner working on his laptop. I couldn't help but feel a little hurt by the fact that he didn't even care about Ben. Cotton, on the other hand, seemed pissed about it.

His brows furrowed as he asked, "And that was it?"

"He followed me out to the car."

"Did he say anything?"

"No. I pulled away before he got a chance."

"Good." Cotton thought for a moment, then asked, "Is there anything else you..."

"Hey, Prez," Wyatt interrupted. "You need to see this."

"What is it?"

Cotton and Stitch stepped over to Wyatt's desk, and the second they looked at the screen, I knew something was terribly wrong. Cotton sounded positively livid as he snarled, "*Fuck*... Is this shit from him?"

"Yes, sir." Wyatt grabbed his phone and held it up. "Got this message when you were talking to Elsie."

As soon as he said my name, Stitch whipped around and ordered, "We're done here. You can go back to your room now."

I nodded nervously, then darted out of the room in a panic.

I'd seen Cotton angry many times before, but this time was different. This time he wasn't just upset over the fact that things hadn't gone the way he expected or someone had mistreated his girls or ol' lady. This time he was angry in a way I'd never seen before. If I hadn't known better, I would've said he was scared, and I'd never seen him scared before.

And that terrified me.

My heart was pounding as I made my way down the hall and back to my room. It was obvious that something bad was going down. Something that included Ben—which made no sense at all. He was just a college student and a psych major at that. It was hard to believe that he was the one who had Cotton and the others so wound up. However, our last encounter was a bit strained, and it had me wondering why he seemed so intent on us spending time together.

The crazy look on his face as he stood in front of my car continued to weigh heavy on my mind as I crawled into bed. I was tired and in dire need of a good night's sleep, but there was no way that was going to happen. I couldn't even close my eyes without seeing that look on Cotton's face, so I got up and headed down the hall to Lacy's room. I knocked, and seconds later, the door creaked open just enough for me to see her flushed face. "Hey, Else. What's up?"

"I couldn't sleep, so... I'm sorry," I stammered. "It's late, and I wasn't thinking. I shouldn't have bothered you."

"It's fine. Is everything okay?"

"Yeah, yeah. Umm... It's just been a long day, and I had a hard time falling asleep."

"Well, where's Bones?" she whispered. "He's the one who should be helping you get to sleep."

"He's working, but it's all good." I feigned a smile as I said, "I'll catch up with you tomorrow."

I silently cursed myself as I turned and started back down the hall. I should've known with all the guys and their families here that Lacy and the girls would have their hands full—literally and figuratively. Regardless, I was still wound tight, and there was no way I was going to be able to fall asleep, so I headed to the kitchen to grab a drink and a bite to eat.

I was just about to pass the family room when I heard Susana's voice. I couldn't make out what she was saying, but it was followed by a round of giggles. I peeked around the corner and saw she and Darby having a glass of wine with Casey, Mia, and Chelsea. I had no doubt that they were using the night to catch up with one another.

I could've joined them.

We were all friends, and I would've enjoyed hearing about what was going on in their lives, but with everything going on, I wasn't in the mood for catching up. I just wanted to grab my snack and get back to bed, so I continued down the hall towards the kitchen.

When I walked in, I was surprised to find Wren sitting alone at the kitchen table. She was wearing her robe and slippers, and she looked lost in her thoughts as she stared off into space. I hated to disturb her, so I tried my best to be quiet as I made my way over to the fridge. I grabbed a soda and some yogurt, then quickly closed the door. I was about to slip back out when Wren looked up and said, "Oh, hey, Elsie. I didn't hear you walk in."

"Hey, Wren," I answered softly. "You doing okay?"

"Yes and no." She shrugged. "You'd think that after all these years, I'd be used to lockdowns and what have you, but they still make me *so nervous*."

"They make me nervous, too. It's one of the reasons I haven't been able to sleep."

"I'm glad to know it's not just me." She patted her hand on the table. "Come over and sit with me a bit. Tell me how things are going with you."

I walked over and sat down next to her, and I immediately felt self-conscious. Even without makeup, Wren was absolutely stunning. She had flawless skin and dark hair and eyes that made her look like she'd just stepped out of some beauty magazine, while I, on the other hand, looked like I'd just rolled out of bed. I tried in vain to brush the many loose strands of hair from my face as I told her, "Things are going okay, I guess."

"And school?" She gave me a warm smile as she asked, "Are things still going well?"

"They are. I'm ready to be done, but it's going great."

"What are your plans after graduation?"

"Well, I've gotta find a job, maybe something in the city, and then, I'll finally start looking for a place of my own. I'm sure the brothers think I've overstayed my welcome."

"You know better than that. They like having you around, especially Wyatt."

"Well, I've really liked being here and having them around, but I can't stay here forever. We both know that."

"And what about you and Wyatt?" Her question caught me off guard. I knew the guys gave him a hard time about me, but I thought it ended there. I had no idea that his mother knew how I felt about him. She must've noticed my surprise, because she quickly added, "Oh, honey. I'm sorry. I didn't mean to be intrusive. I just know he thinks a lot of you, and I was hoping that you felt the same about him."

"I do. *I always have.*" I knew she and Wyatt were very close, and there was a good chance that he'd already told her, but that didn't stop me from saying, "We went out this past weekend, and I think it's safe to say that things went pretty well."

"Really?" Her smile grew wider. "That's great. I had no idea."

"I wouldn't think too much of it. It's just a couple of dates."

"It's more than that. You two have always had a special connection."

"You think?"

"Oh, yes. He's never looked at anyone the way he looks at you, and rightly so. You're a wonderful young woman, Elsie."

"That's really sweet of you to say."

"It's true... You've been through so much." Anguish filled her eyes as she said, "More than any child should ever have to go through, but you didn't let it break you. You fought, and you've kept fighting. That's more than most would do."

"I had some help along the way."

"Yes, and you've helped in return." She placed her hand on mine as she said, "You give Wyatt a calm that he's never had before."

"How?"

"Just by being you." She gave my hand a squeeze. "I see a bright future for you two, and that couldn't please me more."

"It would please me, too, but on nights like these, when I have no idea what's going on, I worry that the future may never come."

"Oh, it will. Stitch and the brothers will make sure of that." She gave me a wink and a smile. "They always do."

"Yeah, I know, but it's hard not to worry."

"Hey." We both turn to find Stitch standing in the doorway, wearing nothing but his wifebeater and boxers. "There a reason why I just woke up in bed alone?"

"I couldn't sleep."

"So you just up and left without saying something?"

"I didn't want to wake you."

"Wake me, baby," he replied, sounding surprisingly sweet. "Always wake me."

"Okay." Wren stood, then reached over and gave my shoulder a quick squeeze. "Thanks for the chat. It meant a lot."

"It meant a lot to me, too."

I watched as Wren walked over to Stitch and gave him a kiss on the lips. He took her by the hand and led her out of the kitchen and down the hall. Even though they were as different as night and day, they worked. They took care of each other in a way that no one else could. As I sat there eating my yogurt, I wondered if there would ever come a time when Wyatt and I would be like them. And the more I thought about it, the more I realized we already were, and that made me smile.

"That must be some really good yogurt," Savage snickered as he walked into the kitchen in his tighty-whities. "What are you doing up so late?"

"Couldn't sleep."

"That seems to be going around." He opened the fridge and pulled out the pitcher of tea. "Something on your mind?"

"Just the usual."

"Hmm." He adjusted himself as he said, "I'd offer you a distraction, but Bones would have my ass."

"Yeah, we wouldn't want that." I chuckled as I got up and tossed my yogurt in the trash. "I think it's time for me to call it a night."

"I'm right behind ya." As we started down the hall, he decided to give it one final go. "If you ever decide to ditch Bones, you know where to find me."

"I do, and I won't."

Without saying anything more, I went into my room and closed the door. I crawled back into bed, and as soon as curled up on my pillow, I found myself wondering if Wyatt was still awake. I reached over and grabbed my phone from the bedside table, then sent him a text message.

Me:

Hey.

Just checking to see if you were awake.

. . .

I waited a few minutes, then sent him another.

Me:
>I guess you're out. I hope you sleep well. Goodnight.

Feeling a bit disappointed, I tossed my phone back onto the table, then laid back on my pillow. I closed my eyes and tried to imagine that we weren't under a lockdown and the guys hadn't asked me all those strange questions about Ben. I told myself that it was a night like any other night, and when the sun rose the following morning, everything would be back to normal.

Only the following day things weren't back to normal.

Not even close.

CHAPTER 14
Bones

"How in the fuck did he get all this shit?" Cotton ran his hand over his face. "Hell, I didn't even know Darby was taking art this semester, and this motherfucker knows the day, the time, the name of the professor, and the exact GPS coordinates of the fucking art building."

"He's got Mia and Wren's schedule, too. He's got them all." It gutted me to hear the anguish in Stitch's voice. I knew what he was feeling. I felt it, too. "What time they go to work. When they go to the gym. Where they get their fucking hair done. He even knows where they get their fucking groceries."

I was just as angry and shaken as my ol' man.

Hell, my blood ran cold when I opened the email and saw the images of my brothers and their families. And I nearly lost it when I saw Elsie's beautiful face on my screen. I scrolled through, noting what the file did and did not include, and there was no doubt it was bad.

I had no idea how bad until we printed it all off.

The file included information about every member of Fury, including their address, their occupation, and daily itinerary. They had the model of the bikes we rode, how long we'd been members, and they had the same information on our significant others and all the children.

I had to admit it was fucking impressive.

He must've spent hours and hours collecting that kind of intel, and I'm not just talking about your basic hacking. He did that and more. He and his men had to have been watching us for months, which explains why we hadn't had any contact with them since the day Q and Rooster were kidnapped and beaten. But it didn't explain why he'd taken them in the first place.

He had all the information.

He didn't need to kidnap and beat them.

It was that thought that had me going back to look over everything we'd collected from the warehouse. I was going over my notes when I heard Cotton ask, "What's this guy trying to prove by having all this shit?"

"He's not trying to prove anything," Stitch

answered. "He's trying to rattle us, and he succeeded. I'm definitely rattled."

"You and me both." Cotton tugged at his thick beard. "I gotta admit, it's been a while since... Anyway, what the hell are we gonna do about this guy?"

"We're gonna burn his ass to the ground. That's what we're gonna do." Stitch's voice grew fierce. "He may have our addresses, but we have his, too! I say we go there and ..."

"I don't think that's a good idea," I interrupted.

"And why not?"

"The only reason why we know who he is and where he lives is because he wanted us to know. That's not the kind of guy you go after with guns blazing," I warned. "We need to know exactly what we're going up against with this guy, or we're gonna fail."

"Fury never fails."

"There's a first time for everything." I could tell by their expressions that my father and president weren't happy about my response. I hated to piss them off, but that didn't make it any less true. "I'm not saying we can't beat this guy. I have no doubt that we can, but we gotta think this thing through."

"He's right. There's no way he did all this on his own." Cotton turned to Big as he said, "You think you and Bones can find out more about our Mr. Davenport? Most importantly, who he's working with?"

"There's another question we need answered."

"Oh?" Cotton turned his attention back to me. "And what's that?"

"Why he had Q and Rooster picked up and questioned." Cotton's brows furrowed as he listened to me say, "He already knew everything he needed to know except one important thing."

"They wanted to know who we are working with?"

"That's right." I motioned my hand over at the table full of files he'd made. "He has everything on us except that."

"So, this is about the business and not some kind of sick revenge tactic?"

"Maybe. Maybe not. It's definitely something to consider while we're looking into him."

"Agreed." Cotton turned back to Stitch as he said, "Time to get our hands on that Ben kid. See what we can find out from him."

"I'll have his address within the hour."

"I'll call church first thing tomorrow. We can fill the boys in on everything then." Cotton had a fatherly tone as he told us, "You boys do what you gotta do, but take the breaks you need to take. I need you both at your best."

"You got it, Prez."

"It's late. I'm gonna go check in with Cass and the

girls. If you find something or need me, you know where to find me."

I nodded, then watched as Cotton and Stitch walked out of the room, leaving Big and me to get to work. I eased over to my desk and turned on my laptop as I asked, "So, where do we start?"

He didn't answer.

He just sat there staring at a sheet of paper.

After several moments, he mumbled, "He's been out there watching them. Josie... Davis... Beck. My woman. My family. It was my job to protect them, and I failed them."

"You didn't fail them. They're here, and they're safe."

"Yeah, but that asshole's been out there watching them."

"It's a background check, brother."

"It's more than that, and *you know it*."

He was right. I knew the kind of effort that went into making those files. Hell, just thinking about the one he had on Elsie brought bile to my throat. I hated that he knew where she was every minute of the day. I hated that Elsie had been used to get closer to us even more.

But I couldn't let myself think about that. Not now.

If I did, I'd completely lose it, and I'd be no good to anyone, including Elsie

For her, I would kill these assholes with my bare hands.

But I'd have to find them first, so I told Big, "He may have the information, but he hasn't used it. At least, not yet. We need to get to him before he tries to do something stupid."

"You're right." He tossed the papers down on the table, then wheeled around to his computer. "We need to find this Ben asshole."

"Yeah, if we can get our hands on him, then Stitch will make him talk. Maybe then we can figure out exactly what we're up against."

We couldn't be sure if he'd used his real name or not, so we pulled his picture from our security feed and ran it through our facial recognition software. It took a couple of tries, but eventually, we were able to ascertain that he was, in fact, Ben Bruton—David Bruton's grandson. I had no idea why Bruton would get his own flesh and blood mixed up in this mess, but it was a decision he would soon regret.

It didn't take long to locate both Ben's permanent address and his campus address, but time was getting away from us. The sun was starting to rise, and it wouldn't be long before everyone would be stirring. With the information in hand, Big stood and started for the door. "You take a break. I'll get this to Stitch and Cotton."

I nodded, but I had no intention of taking a break.

Bruton had reached out to me.

Not once, but twice. And he hadn't said a fucking word to Cotton—the president of Satan's Fury. That meant something, but I had no idea what. I figured he wanted to single me out, and if that was the case, I was about to return the favor. I would find the information the club needed to take him down and turn the tables on him.

I went back to the data I'd pulled from the Interpol server and started looking over Bruton's old cases. I pinned the photographs to the wall, then listed all the names of the people involved and the alleged illegal activity that was being investigated.

I felt like I was grasping at straws,

But I knew in my gut that there was something here.

I just had to find the one singular piece that pulled it all together.

I sat back and just stared at each case, studying the faces and the crimes committed. At first, I couldn't find a damn thing. There didn't seem to be a single connection between the cases, but as I sat there studying all those faces, a pair of crystal blue eyes caught my attention.

I jumped up and rushed over to get a better look. The guy was young, only twenty or so in the picture, but that was over forty years ago. He would've aged a great deal in that length of time.

With that in mind, I placed my hand over his forehead and chin, then tried to imagine the guy with gray hair and wrinkles. That's when it hit me. The man wasn't a fine arts thief. Not even close.

He was Charles Lynskey.

He was a Russian militant who purchased weapons overseas, providing them to those who supported his cause. The discovery led me to check all the names on the wall, making sure the crimes associated with them were legit, and it came as no surprise that they were all bogus. Most had a connection to Al Qaeda and Taliban, and any other militant group who wanted to rise against their government, while others were arms dealers who sold to the highest bidder.

Bruton had investigated all of these men, but for crimes they hadn't committed.

Not that it mattered.

No arrests were ever made.

I was jotting down some thoughts when the door opened, and Stitch entered the room. "You been at this all night?"

"Yeah, but I'm good."

"Don't wanna hear that shit," Stitch fussed. "Get a few hours shut-eye, and then you can get back at it."

"I'm onto something here. I can't just..."

"It'll be waiting for you when you wake up." He motioned his head over to the sofa. "Crash for an hour or two. We'll be back with the grandson by then."

There was no sense in arguing. Stitch wasn't going to let it go, so I got up and made my way over to the sofa. I figured it was better than going all the way back to my room—at least that way, I would be close if anything came up. As soon as I closed my eyes, Stitch turned out the lights and walked out of the room.

I didn't expect to sleep.

My mind was racing with too many unanswered questions, but my curiosity over Bruton's escapades wasn't strong enough to fight against my exhaustion. Eventually, I passed out, and I didn't wake until hours later when I heard Big grumble, "What the fuck?"

I rolled over and found him sitting at my desk, scanning over all the intel I'd gathered on Bruton. He immediately turned to me and asked, "Is this what I think it is?"

"Afraid so." I pulled myself up from the sofa and walked over to him. "Looks like he has connections with arms dealers all over the world."

"Holy shit. I can't believe I missed this." Big

turned to me with a strange look on his face. "You really do have a way with this stuff that I never did."

"You would've found it."

"I'm not so sure. Regardless, I'm glad you pieced it together." His brows furrowed with concern as he asked, "You think this is the reason he's so interested in the club? He wants in on our pipeline?"

"He's the only one who can answer that for certain, but it certainly looks like a strong possibility."

"He's gotta know there's no way in hell that's gonna happen."

"I'm sure he knew we would resist. That's why he decided to use drastic measures." I glanced back over the table full of information on my brothers and their loved ones. "You gotta admit, using our families against us is pretty fucking persuasive."

"But his plan is about to backfire on his ass."

"Yeah, we're gonna show this motherfucker what Fury is all about."

"Damn straight we will." Big motioned his hand over to the wall as he said, "We need to let Cotton and the others in on what you've found."

I nodded, then walked over and started putting everything back into the correct folder. Seeing all the faces of my brothers and their ol' ladies made my stomach twist into a knot, and that knot only grew tighter when I came across Elsie's beautiful face. I wanted to see her, hold her, so I could prove to myself that she was truly okay. Knowing that wasn't an option was getting to me.

Everything was getting to me, and it was getting harder and harder to keep myself in check.

But I had no choice.

My brothers needed me, and I refused to let them down.

Big and I gathered everything we had and carried it to the conference room. We'd just finished setting everything up when Cotton walked in with the rest of the brothers. As soon as they were seated, Big motioned his hand over to me, "Bones is gonna fill you in on a few things. Some aren't gonna be easy to hear, but we both need you to hear him out."

"Is it just me, or does this sound bad?" Two Bit grumbled.

"It certainly isn't good," Cotton responded.

Without saying anything more, Big turned to me and gave me a nod, signaling that it was my turn to speak. Knowing it was going to cause the greatest reaction, I took the files that had been sent to me and distributed the copies throughout the room. As expected, a low, angry rumble filled the room the second the guys started looking over the papers I'd given them.

"These files were sent to my email last night." The

room fell silent as I continued, "I believe they came from David Bruton, a man many of you know as the high school history teacher."

"Come again?" Diesel snapped.

"I know it's hard to believe, but it's true."

I turned to the computer screen mounted on the wall and pulled up the information I'd collected on Bruton, including how I'd discovered that he was actually Carl Davenport. The guys never said a word. They simply sat there in complete bewilderment as I told them how he once worked for Interpol and how his cases provided him with connections to some very powerful men.

"If he has these kinds of connections, what does he want with us?" Maverick asked. "And why now? What's changed over the past forty years?"

"I'm still trying to figure that out," I admitted. "I'm hoping his grandson will have some answers for us. Stitch and Wrath are out looking for him now."

"And what are you expecting us to do until then?" Smokey was known for being calm and rational, especially since he married MJ, but he sounded neither calm nor rational as he snarled, "'Cause I'm not just gonna sit here and wait for this motherfucker to come after my ol' lady and kids."

"I understand your frustration. Hell, I'm frustrated, too." The tension in the room was crackling around me, causing the knot in my stomach to grow tighter. I felt like I was teetering on the edge as I told him, "But we don't know what kind of manpower this guy has got. It could just be him and a couple of guys, or he could have a whole fucking army. We don't need to make a move until we know more, and we won't know more until we get our hands on the grandson."

A war was brewing.

And I feared it would bring a battle like we'd never seen before.

CHAPTER 15
Elsie

I thought I was dreaming, that I hadn't really felt the bed dip as Wyatt slipped into bed next to me. I thought the scent of his cologne and the rough bristles of his day-old beard against my neck were just figments of my imagination. It wasn't until I felt the warmth of his hand trail up my thigh that I realized it was really him. My breath caught as his fingers curled around the band of my panties and pulled them down over my hips. "Wyatt?"

He didn't answer.

Instead, his hands reached for the hem of my nightgown and gently pulled it over my head. I wanted to protest and force him to talk to me, but it felt so good to have him so close. I'd missed him. I'd missed his touch and his mouth against my skin, and I just couldn't tell him to stop. He settled himself between my legs, then brushed his tongue roughly against me, causing my back to arch against the mattress.

I knew something was wrong. I could see it in his eyes, but he refused to speak. I wanted him to know that he could open up to me, so I tried once again. "Wyatt, is something wrong? Talk to me."

Giving no response whatsoever, he continued to torment me with his mouth. There was something different about the way he touched me. It wasn't his usual sensual caress. It was rough and demanding like a man possessed, and while it felt incredible, there was something off about it.

I tried to resist. I didn't want to come when he was being so cold and distant, but the second his warm, wet mouth pressed against me, I was unable to hold back. Every nerve in my body started to tingle, and just when I thought I couldn't take it anymore, his fingers delved inside me, twisting and turning as he dragged them across my g-spot. Jolts of pleasure surged through me as he brought me to the edge, making it impossible to resist.

My hands dropped to his head, my fingers tangling in his hair as that familiar tingling sensation began to churn in my abdomen. I clamped down around his fingers as my release ripped through me, leaving me in a complete daze.

I was still trying to gather my senses when Wyatt

started to unbuckle his belt. Hoping to draw his attention, I whispered, "Wyatt."

He didn't answer, so I said his name again, louder this time. "Wyatt."

When he still didn't answer, I quickly sat up and scooted out of his reach, tugging the covers up to my chest. His eyes narrowed with a mix of anger and confusion. I quickly shook my head and told him, "No, Wyatt. Not like this."

"What?"

"Not like this," I repeated. "You're not talking to me. It's like you don't even know it's me..."

He didn't respond, and it hurt my feelings even more.

My voice trembled as I told him, "If you're just wanting to get off, then go get one of the other girls because I'm not interested."

"It's not like that."

"Well, it certainly feels that way." A tear trickled down my cheek as I told him, "It hurts me when you won't talk to me, Wyatt, especially when we're like this."

I hoped he would apologize or, at the very least, explain what was going on inside his head, but he didn't say a word. He simply stood there staring at me with a storm of emotion raging in his eyes. I wanted to be there for him, but not like this—not unless he opened up and talked to me. He stood there for a moment longer, then turned and started for the door. "I'm sorry."

"Wyatt! Wait!"

I jumped off the bed and rushed after him, but I was too late. He was already out the door and halfway down the hall. I would've gone after him, but I wasn't dressed and had no desire to give the brothers an eyeful. Flustered, I slammed my door and got back in bed. I sifted through my blankets, and once I found my nightgown, I slipped it over my head and nestled under my covers.

I loved Wyatt.

I'd loved him for years.

He'd always been there for me when I needed him, and I wanted to do the same for him. But to do that, I needed him to talk to me, not shut me out. I tried to give him a moment, hoping in time he would show me the tenderness he'd shown me the first time we slept together, and it was impossible not to be hurt when he didn't. I hated that he seemed so closed off, so lost, when he touched me.

I hated it even more that he'd left. I waited for over an hour, hoping that he would eventually come back. When he didn't, I decided to take matters into my own hands. I got out of bed, put on some clothes, and charged down the hall to Wyatt's room. I tapped on the door, but there was no answer. I knocked a little harder, but yet again, no answer.

I was beginning to think that he'd taken my harsh words to heart and had gone to hook up with one of the club girls when I heard a faint hum coming from inside his room. I turned the doorknob, and to my surprise, it wasn't locked. I eased it open and whispered into the dark, "Wyatt?"

There was no answer, but I could still hear the muffled hum in the corner. I opened the door a little wider, letting the light from the hall fill the room. That's when I spotted Wyatt sitting at his desk, his hand covering his eyes, and he was wearing a pair of headphones. I closed the door and quietly made my way over to him. I placed my hands on his headphones, and an old rock song blasted from the earpieces as I slipped them off his head.

He turned off the music, then whipped around with a start. "Elsie?"

"Yeah, it's me." I reached across his desk and turned on the lamp. "I wanted to make sure you're okay."

"I'm better now." He placed his hands on my hips and tugged me closer, and anguish filled his eyes as he whispered, "I'm sorry about earlier."

"What exactly was that?"

"It was nothing... I was just in my head."

"In your head about what?"

"You." He lowered his forehead to my chest and sighed. "I can't take the idea of something happening to you."

"Nothing's gonna happen to me, Wyatt." I ran my fingers through his thick hair. "I'm right here. I'm not going anywhere."

"I wish I could believe that."

"You have no reason not to." I placed my hand under his chin, forcing him to look up at me. "You have to know how I feel about you."

"But why?"

"Because you gave me a reason to get up and face the day." Tears stung my eyes as I told him, "I'd lost everything, Wyatt. My family. My home. And there were times when I thought about giving in to the heartbreak, but then, I'd see you. I don't know how you always knew, but you never failed to be there when I needed you the most."

"You do the same for me."

"I'd say we're pretty lucky to have one another."

"No doubt." A lopsided grin crept across his handsome face. "You remember the day I wiped out on Hayes' dirt bike?"

"How could I forget? You almost killed yourself that day."

"Yeah, it was pretty bad. I tried to hide from everyone, especially my mother. I'd barely returned to my room when you came rushing up behind me." He shook his head, "Pretty sure the scolding you gave me was worse than the one my mother would've given me."

I gave him a playful nudge and giggled, "Well, you deserved it... *and more.*"

"You're probably right."

"I'm absolutely right." That worried crease between his brow had finally started to fade, so I took the opportunity to say, "You wouldn't talk to me. You were so closed off. It was like you were there, but you weren't."

"I know, and I'm sorry about that." He stood and placed his hands on my hips. "I should've dealt with my shit before ever coming to your room."

"No, I want to be the person you come to, but you gotta talk to me, like you used to. You can't shut me out." I could see the wheels turning in his head, so I added, "Don't misunderstand. I know you can't discuss club stuff and all that, but I'm here for anything else, just like I've always been. And you've always been for me. That's why we work. We're here for the good and the bad. And that's the way I always want it to be."

The words barely left my mouth when he leaned forward and lowered his lips to mine, kissing me tenderly. My entire body tingled as he delved deeper into my mouth. I'd never felt anything so intense, so full of desire, as we clung to each other like we were taking our last breath. He released my mouth just long enough to whisper, "I don't deserve you. But I can't let you go... I need you too much."

"I need you, too."

His eyes never left mine as I reached for his shirt and began unbuttoning it slowly. I loved how he looked at me like I was the sun, and everything revolved around me. His lips brushed against mine, but not gently like before. Instead, it was hot, passionate, and demanding. I gasped when he lifted me up, cradling me close to his chest as he carried me over to the bed.

He carefully lowered my feet to the floor, and a wave of anticipation washed over me when he reached for the hem of my t-shirt and eased it over my head. Wasting no time, he slipped his hands around my back and undid my bra, letting it fall to the floor. After taking a moment to appraise me, he leaned forward and covered my mouth with a hungry kiss. In that instant, everything around me seemed to slip away.

My chest tightened when he whispered, "I wish I knew how to tell you what you mean to me."

"You don't have to say the words." I placed my

palm on his cheek and whispered, "I feel it when you touch me... when you look at me."

The words had barely left my mouth when his lips came crashing down on mine.

The caress of his lips was magic, making me feel like I was floating on air. The tips of his fingers trailed along my spine, and I arched towards him, seeking the heat of his touch.

I could feel a fire burning deep inside me, smoldering as it spread through my body. It had started with just a spark, but I could feel it building, intensifying with every touch of his hand. A rush of heat rolled against my skin as he released my mouth and looked down at me. He stood there silently staring at me, appraising me.

Everything about him seduced my senses.

His touch.

His smell.

The way he looked at me.

I'd never wanted anything like I wanted him, and the way his eyes filled with lust and love when he looked at me only made me want him more. Seconds later, I was on my back with his rough, impatient hands roaming all over my body. His need was building with each kiss, every touch, and he was losing all sense of control.

"You're finally mine... All mine."

Hearing the need in his voice sent a wave of desire coursing through my veins. It burned deep, nearly taking my breath away. I lay there staring up at him, breathless and aching for his touch. When I finally came to my senses, I smiled and said, "I've always been yours."

My breath caught when his hands slid down to the waistband of my sweats and lowered them down my hips. He ran one hand between my legs while his other hand cupped my breast, the rough pad of his thumb brushing across my nipple. His every touch added fuel to the fire burning inside me.

Impatient for more, I reached for his belt, letting him know that I was just as eager as he was. Once it was undone, he slowly stood up, dropping them to the floor, then reached into his side drawer for a condom. A spark of mischief flashed through his eyes as he slowly slipped it on. He knew the effect he had on me, and he loved it, but no more than I did. Heat rushed over me as my eyes roamed over his perfectly defined abs and pronounced V.

He was beautiful, and he was mine.

All mine.

A deep growl vibrated through his chest as he lowered himself onto the bed and settled between my legs. He brushed against my center, teasing me relentlessly before he finally thrust deep inside me. My head fell back as I gasped for air, my fingers pressing into his back, and my entire body gripped with heat.

He moved slowly, meticulously at first, but then his pace quickened, becoming more demanding and intense with each shift of his hips.

The muscles in my abdomen began to tighten as my legs drew up beside him. My hands curled around his back as I held on to him, bracing myself for the wave of pleasure that I could feel growing inside me. His steady rhythm never faltered until we both reached our climax. He lowered himself on top of me with the heat of his breath on my neck, and he didn't move. He just lay there, holding me close.

Once he'd caught his breath, he tossed his condom in the trash, then lowered himself down on the bed next to me. "Unbelievable."

"It was *pretty incredible*."

"No, it was more than that." Wyatt kept his eyes trained on the ceiling as he admitted, "It's never been like this before."

"What? The fooling around?"

"Yeah." His eyes locked on mine. "You know I've been with other women?"

I cringed at the thought, and it didn't go unnoticed.

"Never mind... Bad timing."

"No, I told you I wanted you to be able to talk to me, so talk. Tell me what you were thinking."

"It never felt like this with them."

"Is that a good thing?"

"It's a very good thing."

"Well, that's good to know. But just so you know, I really don't like thinking about you being with other women."

"Why? You jealous?"

"*Maybe.*"

"You are." A proud smile crossed his face. "I like you being jealous."

I didn't respond.

I simply cocked my brow and glared at him until he started laughing.

"Okay. Okay. Message received." His laughter faded as he rolled to his back. "If it makes you feel any better, I wasn't exactly happy about you going out with that Ben fella."

"You had no reason to be jealous about him. I should've never gone out with him." I eased up on my elbow and glanced down at him as I asked, "Did he do something to the club? Is he the reason why we're in lockdown?"

"You know I can't talk about that."

"But I'm the one who brought him here."

"You got nothing to do with what's going on."

"Then, why did Cotton ask me all those questions about Ben?"

"*Elsie.*"

"Fine." I dropped back down on my pillow. "But I know he did something, and I would hate to think that he was able to do whatever he did because of me."

"Already told you." His tone grew stern. "You have nothing to do with this."

I could tell that he was becoming aggravated, and that was the last thing I wanted, especially after the moment we'd just shared. So, I did the only thing I could. I dropped it. I curled up next to him with a sigh. The room fell silent, but only for a moment.

"Do you remember the Thanksgiving we had out at Cotton's place?" I didn't have to look at him to know he was smiling as he said, "All the kids were riding horses, and Darby and Susana talked you into riding with them?"

"Are you referring to the day that I rode a horse for *the very first time in my life* and got thrown off into a huge mud puddle?"

"Yeah, that'd be the one."

"I haven't thought about that for years. I was absolutely mortified," I groaned. "Susana and Darby were such great riders. They made it look *soooo* easy, and I thought for sure that I could do it. *WRONG*! I'd barely taken the reins when that damn horse took off like a bolt of lightning."

A mischievous smile swept across his face as he snickered, "*Ooohhh, I remember.*"

"It wasn't funny, Wyatt."

"*Ummm, yeah.*" He continued to chuckle. "It was funny. Damn. Every inch of you was covered in mud. I still don't know how you managed that."

"I fell! Ugh! You're such an asshole." I gave him a nudge with my elbow. "I didn't laugh at you after your dirt bike wreck when you were whining about your little booboo on your elbow."

"I had to get fifteen stitches. It was not a little booboo."

"But did you die?" I sassed. "'Cause you certainly acted like you were going to. I've never heard such."

"I got a scar," he huffed. "All you had was a couple of bruises that faded by the end of the week."

"You're right. The bruises did fade, but I broke my tail bone and I had to sit on that stupid round pillow for weeks."

"Oh, yeah. I forgot about the pillow." He started chuckling again. "I never did understand why you got a hot pink one. There was no missing it."

"It was the only color they had!"

"I would've had to go without."

"You say that now, but break your tailbone, and then, we'll talk."

We lay there for hours, cuddling and sharing old stories, and I fell asleep in his arms, feeling like everything was right in the world. But sadly, it wasn't a feeling that would last. At the time, I didn't know it, but my whole world was about to be turned upside down, and I would be forced to make a decision I never thought I would make.

CHAPTER 16
Bones

"I just got word from Stitch," Cotton announced. "They've gone to the addresses you gave them. His shit is still at the apartment, but there's been no sign of the kid. Same for his folk's place."

"Fuck." Big turned to me as he said, "We can try tracking his phone."

"Gotta have a number to do that."

"What about Elsie?" Cotton asked. "You think she has it?"

"Maybe, but if I ask her for his number, it's only gonna bring up more questions—questions I can't answer."

"She's not new to this kind of thing."

"*No, but this is different*."

"What if I tell her I need her phone?" Big

suggested. "I can say it's an update or something. For that matter, I can give her a new burner and tell her we're trashing the old one."

"That could work. Just hate lying to her."

"You won't be the one lying. *I will.*"

"Yeah, whatever. Just get the damn phone and let's find this guy."

Big nodded, then grabbed a new burner phone from the lockbox and started out of the room. As soon as he was out of earshot, Cotton stepped over to me and asked, "How you holding up?"

"I'm good."

"Word is that you and Else are finally making a go of it."

"Yeah, I finally pulled my head out of my ass."

"Good to hear. She's a good girl, and her father was a hell of a man. I owe him a lot."

"I'll do right by her, Prez. You've got my word on that."

"I have no doubt that you will, son." Concern marked his face as he asked, "You handling this thing with her?"

"I'm doing the best I can. It's tough keeping stuff from her, but I know it's for her own good."

"It is tough, and it only gets tougher. But, in the end, you'll be saving her a whole lotta heartache. Trust me on that."

"Understood."

Before either of us could say anything more, Big rushed into the room and announced, "I got it."

"She suspect anything?"

"Nah," Big tossed me the phone. "I took Lacy's too, so she didn't think anything of it."

"Good deal."

I opened her phone, and a tinge of guilt prickled over me as I started looking through her contacts. I hated invading her privacy, especially after the conversation we'd just had, but I didn't have a choice. I started with the basic alphabetical search but didn't find any contact information under the name Ben. When I started searching for Bruton, I noticed that she had created nicknames for each of her contacts.

They ranged from Papa Bear and Twinkle Toes to Boss Man and Fashionista. Some were easy to pick up on like Cotton was listed as Prez and Lacy was Queen B, but others, like Lil' Grumps and Tater Tot, weren't so easy. For those, I had no choice but to look through her messages and try to decipher who they came from. I started with the first message, *Stud Muffin*, and was pleased to see it was from me.

I might've even smiled at the fact.

Noting the change in my demeanor, Big cleared his throat and asked, "Something we need to see over there?"

"Nope."

"You sure about that?"

"Yeah, I'm sure. Now, pipe down," I fussed. "I'm trying to work over here."

"Um-hmm."

Knowing I didn't have time to mess around, I turned my focus back to the messages and skipped down to the next name I didn't recognize. It took me a few lines to figure out that *Lil Grumps* was actually Makayla, and *Tator Tot* was a girl from one of her classes. I continued down the stream of messages, but none seemed to be from Ben. I was beginning to think that they'd never actually texted until I scrolled down to the name *Donnie Dipshit*.

I'd never heard her speak of anyone named Donnie, so I was a bit intrigued as I opened his message. It didn't take long to realize that Donnie the Dipshit was actually our boy, Ben. I felt a sense of unease as I continued down the thread and saw that it wasn't just a couple of messages. They'd spoken often.

Even though they dropped off after their last day, I felt a tug of jealousy when I saw the various flirty exchanges. I hated the idea of her even looking at another guy, much less flirting with him, and I hated it even more that the asshole had used her to make a move against the club. It was something he would soon regret.

"I got it."

Big stepped over to his laptop and ordered, "Give me the number."

I called it out to him, and within minutes, he turned to Cotton and said, "We got him."

"Where the hell is he?"

"Just over two hours from here," Big answered. "At an apartment in Tacoma."

"Damn." Cotton whipped out his phone as he ordered, "Send me the exact location."

As soon as Big gave him the address, Cotton forwarded it to Stitch and Wrath. Ben might've been farther away than we'd hoped, but it was only a matter of time before his nightmares became his reality in Stitch's playroom. As soon as he was certain Stitch had received the message, he stuck his phone back in his pocket as he said, "We'll need to keep an eye on his location and make sure it doesn't change."

"Won't be a problem." Big turned to me as he asked, "Have you checked out Bruton's financials?"

"Not yet, but it definitely needs to be done." I stepped over to his desk. "Shouldn't be hard to find his banking information. Just need to see where the city deposits his check."

"Already on it."

Big started typing away at his keyboard, and I knew it wouldn't be long before he had access to all of

Bruton's accounts. Cotton and I were watching him work when there was a tap at the door. I walked over and opened it, and I was surprised to find Elsie standing in the hallway. She was wearing jeans and a hoodie, and she had her backpack on her shoulder. A warm smile crossed her face as she said, "Hey. I hate to bother you, but I wanted to let you know I was heading out. I have to get to class."

"You got a prospect or brother going with you?"

"Yeah, Torch and Alto are following me over."

"When's your class?"

"I have one at eleven and another at two. We should be back around four."

"And these are classes you can't miss?"

"No." Her brows furrowed. "I'm too close to the end of the term to be skipping."

"Understood." I stepped into the hall and closed the door behind me. "Go straight to class and stay close to Torch. I don't want you taking any chances."

"I'm gonna be fine, Wyatt. It's just a couple of classes. And they are on campus with tons of people."

"Yeah, well, the tons of people isn't exactly a positive."

"It's the same people who are always there."

"Again, not exactly a positive."

"Well, Torch and Alto will be there to keep an eye on things, so stop worrying." She eased up on her tiptoes and gave me a quick kiss. "I'll see you when I see you. Don't work too hard."

With that, she turned and started towards the back door. As soon as she was out of sight, I stuck my head back into the office and announced, "I'm going to grab a cup of coffee. You guys need anything?"

"I'm good," Big answered.

"I'll take a refill." Cotton reached over and grabbed his empty cup from the table. "Black. Two sugars."

"You got it."

I grabbed his cup, then headed to the kitchen. When I walked in, I was pleased to see that someone had just brewed a fresh pot. I refilled Cotton's cup, then filled one of my own. I was about to head back to the office when I heard Lacy say, "Hey, Bones. How's it going?"

"It's going. You?"

"The same." She stepped over and started pouring herself some coffee. "You seen Elsie?"

"She just left for class."

"Oh, she went?" she asked, sounding surprised. "I wouldn't have thought you guys would let her go with the lockdown and all."

"She didn't go alone."

"Oh, that makes sense." Lacy studied me for a moment, then asked, "So, you and her are kind of a thing now, huh?"

"You could say that."

"Good." A somber look crossed her face as she said, "I always thought you guys would end up together."

"Seems you aren't the only one."

"I wouldn't figure so... You know, she deserves someone who will be good to her." Lacy's eyes narrowed. "So, be good to her 'cause we know she'll be good to you."

"I plan on it. You don't have to worry about that."

"I'm gonna hold you to that." She lifted her cup and smiled as she started out of the kitchen. "Have a good one, Bones."

"You too, Lace."

As soon as she was gone, I grabbed Cotton's cup of coffee and mine, then started back to the office. When I walked back in, I found Cotton and Big staring intently at Big's laptop screen. As I started over to them, I heard Prez grumble, "This doesn't make any sense."

"He's gotta have another account that we aren't seeing."

"You'd think, but where?"

"It's gotta be an offshore account," I told them as I made my way over to Big's desk. "It'd make sense seeing that most of his clients are overseas."

"But it doesn't explain how he's paying his folks here."

"He could be using the same offshore account." I walked over to my desk and turned on my computer as I continued, "But we won't know for sure until we find those accounts."

I pulled up the files I'd gathered from Interpol and started searching for Carl Davenport's tax id, thinking it might help us locate those offshore accounts. I knew it was a long shot. He'd already taken the measures to change his name and even took on a new identity. It only made sense that he would get a fake social security number and everything in between, but I hoped there might be some connection between the two.

I was busy searching for something that might help us locate his offshore accounts when I heard Big announce, "The kid is on the move."

"Where's he headed?"

"Not sure." Big was silent for a moment, then added, "Looks like he's headed north."

"I'll message Stitch. Keep an eye on him, and let me know when you have a better idea of where he's going."

I was too wrapped up in finding Bruton's accounts to think much about Ben and his shenanigans. Besides, I knew it was only a matter of time before Stitch and

Wrath had him in their clutches, and then, it would be over for the douchebag.

I kept hammering away, and it wasn't long before I found a possible lead. After some cross-referencing, I knew I'd found something. I became solely focused on what I was working on, ignoring Big and Cotton talking behind me until I heard Big say, "Looks like he's headed to the university."

"What?"

"I might be wrong, but it's looking like he's headed for campus." Big turned to face me as he asked, "That's where he met up with Elsie, right?"

"Yeah, they have some classes together."

"Then, we need to get in touch with Torch and give him a heads up."

"On it."

Cotton took out his phone and dialed Torch's number. As luck would have it, he didn't answer. He tried again, but nothing. "I'm sending him a message. You call Elsie and give her a heads up."

I nodded, then grabbed my phone from my pocket. I dialed her number, but it went straight to voice mail. I tried two more times, but she never picked up. I was becoming anxious when Cotton told us, "I got him. They are at the student union, and all is good. There's been no sign of Ben."

"Tell them to bring Elsie home." I could feel myself

becoming unhinged and tried my best to remain calm as I told him, "The last thing we need is this guy fucking with her."

"That's not gonna happen." Cotton was staring down at his phone as he told me, "Stitch and Wrath are close on his trail."

"I don't want her anywhere near this guy, Prez."

"Then, tell her to get her ass home."

I nodded, then sent her a message.

Me:

Come home.

Elsie:

I'm on my way to class.

Me:

Don't care.
Need you to get home.

I waited a moment but got no response.

So, I messaged her again.

. . .

Me:

Elsie, no fucking around.
I need you to come home.

Me:

Elsie?

I tossed my phone down on the table as I grumbled, "Fuck."

"No luck?"

"Fuck no." I ran my hand over my face with frustration. "She's either already in class, or she's fucking ignoring me."

"Torch just messaged and said she made it inside."

"*Fuck.*"

"He'd have to be a real dumbass to pull something on that campus." Big was trying to reassure me, but it wasn't working—not even when he added, "And Stitch and Wrath are right on his tail. You don't gotta worry. He won't get the chance to get close to her."

I wish that was the case.

Sadly, it wasn't.

CHAPTER 17
Elsie

I knew Wyatt was worried about me coming to class, but I didn't know how worried until I received his message about me coming back to the clubhouse. Under any other circumstances, I would've just done what he said and headed back, but I had to get my project assignment for the following week. And I had Torch and Alto watching my every move.

They even walked with me up the front steps of my building and watched as I headed inside. They were taking every precaution—not that they needed to. There were people everywhere, including campus security. I felt completely safe, which was why I replied to Wyatt that I was on my way to class and put my phone on silent. I shoved it into my back pocket and continued down the hall.

I was just about to step into class when I felt someone's hand on my arm, and I was jerked back. Seconds later, I was in a small, enclosed place with very little light. I took a quick look around and saw that I was in a supply closet with a man wearing a black hoodie. I immediately started punching, kicking, and screaming at him but stopped when he snarled, *"Stop, Elsie! It's me."*

"Ben?" I gasped. "What the hell? What are you doing?"

"I came to warn you." He eased his hoodie back, revealing his unshaven face and tired eyes. It looked like he hadn't slept or bathed for days. "These men you live with aren't who you think they are."

"What the hell are you talking about?"

"They are dangerous. They're criminals." He grabbed my arm, tugging me closer as he warned, "You gotta get away from them."

"Have you lost your mind?"

"I'm sorry I had to pull you in here, but it's the only way I could talk to you." He pointed his hand towards the door. "I couldn't get close to you with those two friends of yours following your every move."

"Okay. You have my attention. Now, tell me what the hell you want."

"You're in danger. You gotta come with me," he pleaded. "I'll take you somewhere safe."

"I'm not going anywhere with you." I gave him a hard shove. "You need to get the hell out of here and never speak to me again."

"I'm not leaving without you, Elsie." He inched his hoodie up, revealing the pistol harnessed at his waist. "You're coming with me."

Until that moment, I'd been too angry to realize that I was in danger and should be scared. There was no doubt about that now. Panic washed over me as I stammered, "You don't... you don't want to do this, Ben."

"No, I don't, but you've left me no choice." His voice turned menacing as he growled, "There are questions that have to be answered, and you're gonna help me answer them."

"What the fuck are you talking about?"

"I don't have time for this shit." His tone grew fierce as he snarled, "You're coming with me, and then you can answer all his stupid questions."

This was bad.

This was very, very bad.

I knew the guys were right outside. I also knew the likelihood of Ben getting past them was slim, but he had a gun and he looked just rattled enough to use it. I needed him to settle down, so I kept my tone steady as I said, "I don't know what you're talking about."

"It doesn't matter. We just gotta go."

"But how? You can't exactly walk out of here with a gun at my back."

"That's exactly what I'm gonna do." He eased the door open and peered through the crack, checking to see if anyone was in the hall. My stomach dropped when he took hold of my arm and ordered, "Let's go."

"Ben, please."

"I don't have time for games, Elsie. Move your ass or you'll make me do something we'll both regret."

My mind was racing as I stepped out in the hall. I knew I couldn't leave with him, so I started looking around, searching for someone who might be able to help me.

There was no one.

Classes had already started, and the halls were clear.

It was just me and Ben, leaving me no choice but to try and talk some sense into him. "This is a bad idea, Ben. You have to know that."

"It didn't have to be this way." He looked down at me with emotion-filled eyes. "If you'd just listened to me, I could've helped you. I could've prevented all this. Now, you'll have to deal with him."

The eerie tone in his voice and the second mention of ***him*** had me spiraling. My pulse quickened and my throat tightened, making it difficult to speak as I muttered, "Deal with who?"

He didn't answer.

Instead, he opened the glass door and shoved me through it, then started forcing me towards the parking lot. We hadn't gotten far when Stitch stepped up behind us. I'd barely blinked when he had his hand on Ben's throat, squeezing it tightly as he pinned him against the building. "This is how it's gonna go. The girl is gonna walk away, and you and I are gonna take a little walk out to my truck."

"I'm not going anywhere with you."

"I got a .45 that says different." Stitch kept his hand at Ben's throat as he rammed the barrel of his gun into Ben's chest. "Elsie, go. Torch and Alto are waiting for you."

Without any hesitation, I did as Stitch ordered and stepped free from Ben's grasp. Wrath was standing at Stitch's side keeping watch, and he was quick to motion me in Torch's direction. He was standing at the bottom of the steps and was talking on the phone.

As I made my way down to him, I was relieved to see that there were only a few students in the area, and they all were preoccupied with their phones or each other.

Concern marked Torch's face as he rushed up to me and asked, "You okay?"

"Yeah, I'm fine."

"Good." He took me by the arm and led me out to

the parking lot as he spoke into the phone, "We got her. She's good."

There was a brief pause, and then he replied, "Yeah, we're headed back now."

He hung up the phone and shoved his phone in his back pocket. When we got out to his truck, he opened the door and waited as I got inside. Before he closed the door, I asked, "What about my car?"

"Alto will drive it back for you." He held out his hand as he said, "Give me the keys."

Again, I didn't argue.

I gave him the keys, and he tossed them over to Alto. Minutes later, we were all on the road headed back to the clubhouse, and for the first time, I had a second to think about what had just transpired. I'd been so wrong about everything. I'd thought Ben was just a regular guy, but today proved that wasn't the case.

I had no idea what was going on between him and the brothers, but there was no doubt that he was in trouble. He'd come to kidnap me, and he would've succeeded if Stitch hadn't shown up. And while I was relieved he came when he did, I couldn't figure out how he knew we were in that storage closet. I knew it was doubtful that Torch would give me a clear answer, but I had to ask, "What were Stitch and Wrath doing in the communications building? Were they there for me or for Ben?"

"You know I can't answer that." He kept his eyes trained on the road as he added, "Best to forget any of this happened."

"But it did happen."

"Elsie."

"What about Ben? What's going to happen to him?"

"None of your concern."

"How can you say that?" I huffed. "I'm the one he had locked up in a storage closet! I'm the one he threatened with a gun!"

"He did what?"

"He had a gun." My throat tightened as I told him, "He told me he was taking me with him and that I could answer his questions."

"Answer whose questions?"

"I have no idea."

The more I thought about my exchange with Ben, the more rattled I became. I'd really messed up. I should've listened to Wyatt. I should've gone home like he asked me to, but I was too damn worried about a stupid class to listen, and it could've cost me. Thankfully, Stitch came before things got out of hand.

I didn't bother asking Torch any more questions.

There was no point.

He didn't know any more than I did, and even if he did, he wouldn't tell me.

When we got back to the clubhouse, Torch led me inside and said, "I'm sure Cotton will want a word with you. Until then, go to your room and stay put."

I nodded, then did as he'd ordered and went straight to my room. I'd barely closed my door when it flew open, and Wyatt charged inside.

"Are you okay?" He wrapped his arms around me, hugging me tightly as he asked, "Did he hurt you?"

"No, he didn't hurt me... I'm okay, Wyatt."

"Are you sure?"

He held my gaze as he brought his hands up to my face and slowly brushed his thumb across my bottom lip. He slowly leaned closer, and warmth rushed over me when I felt a slight tickle from his beard against my jaw. He was so close, just inches away, but he didn't kiss me. Instead, he hovered over me, lingering above me as he whispered, "I don't know what I would do if something happened to you."

Without saying anything more, he lowered his lips to mine in a possessive kiss. His arm slipped around my waist, pulling me over to him as he delved deeper, claiming me with his mouth. I'd never felt anything so intense, so full of emotion, as we clung to each other like we were taking our last breath. I felt safe in his arms, like he would do anything in the world to protect me, and I immediately missed the sensation when he eased back, breaking our embrace.

"Cotton's gonna want a word with you."

"Yeah, Torch already told me, but there's not much to tell."

"He'll want to hear it all the same."

"I figured as much." I inhaled a deep breath, then asked, "Do you think there's any way we can just get it over with?"

"Yeah." He reached down and took my hand in his. "He's waiting for us in his office."

"Okay."

Wyatt led me out of the room, and together, we made our way down the hall to Cotton's office. When we walked in, he was sitting at his desk talking to Guardrail, and neither of them appeared to be in the best of moods. In fact, they looked fit to be tied. His expression softened, and Cotton sounded sincerely worried as he asked, "You okay?"

"Yes, sir. I'm fine."

"Good. You had us worried there for a minute." His eyes narrowed as he asked, "You wanna tell me what happened today?"

"Yeah, sure, but like I told Wyatt, there's not much to tell."

"Still wanna hear it from you."

"Yes, sir." Wyatt gave my hand a gentle squeeze as I

told him, "He pulled me into the closet and started saying all this crazy stuff about you guys being dangerous and that I needed to get away from you. I told him he was off his rocker, and I might've pushed him. That's when he showed me his gun and told me he was taking me with him."

Cotton glanced over at Guardrail, then back to me. "Any idea where he was planning to take you?"

"No, sir. He didn't say."

"Anything else?"

"He mentioned something about me answering *his questions*, but I have no idea who he was talking about. He forced me out of the closet, and when we stepped out of the building, that's when Stitch appeared. And our conversation ended there." I nervously bit down on my bottom lip before saying, "I'm really sorry. I should've listened to Wyatt and gone back to the clubhouse the second he texted me."

"Yes, you should have." His tone turned fatherly as he scolded, "Things could've turned out very differently today, and none..."

Before he could finish his thought, Two Bit stepped into the office and announced, "He's ready."

Cotton nodded, then turned to Wyatt. "We're done here. Take her back to her room and then come find us."

"You got it."

With that, we all filed out of the office and into the hall. Cotton and Guardrail followed Two Bit towards the back door while Wyatt and I headed back to my room. When we walked in, I looked up at Wyatt and asked, "I don't guess you're gonna tell me where you all are going?"

"No, but I can tell you that I won't be long." He leaned down and kissed me on the forehead. "Try to stay out of trouble until I get back."

"I'll do my best."

He took one last look at me, then turned and walked out of the room. I won't deny that I wanted him to stay. I wanted him to hold me in his arms and calm the storm of thoughts that were racing through my head. But sadly, it didn't matter what I wanted. The brothers needed him, and that was that.

My time would come.

I just hoped it would be sooner rather than later.

CHAPTER 18
Bones

I thought a lot of Stitch.
  I looked up to him.
  I respected him.

He was my father in every way that counted.

But I would never understand how he could do the things he did to people in his playroom. He strung them up and tortured them in unimaginable ways—whatever it took to get them to talk. Sometimes it just took a simple threat. For others, it took hours, *even days*, of horrific beatings and heinous acts to get them to start talking.

As I stood there staring through the two-way glass, I couldn't help but wonder what lay in store for Ben. His arms were bound over his head, his feet barely touching the ground, and his eyes were wide with fear. I couldn't blame him for being terrified. Stitch and

Wrath stood before him, arms crossed with angry scowls on their faces, and with his gun nowhere in sight, he was helpless to defend himself.

It didn't help matters that there was a variety of tools splayed out on the table. He knew what was in store for him, which was why he told Stitch, "I wasn't gonna hurt her. I would never hurt her."

"I'm gonna give you a piece of advice here, kid." Stitch stepped closer to him. "Don't speak until spoken to. You got that?"

Ben nodded. "Yeah, I got it."

We all watched as Stitch stepped over and said something to Wrath. While it would be up to a club vote, he was priming him as a possible replacement as the club's enforcer. It was a role he'd had since I'd met him, and while it would be hard to see him go, I understood why he was ready to step down. His role in the club was an important one, but it was also a trying one that left him mentally and physically exhausted.

After their brief exchange, Stitch turned his focus back to Ben. "Tell me what you wanted with the girl."

"Nothing. I was just..."

Before he could finish his thought, Stitch drew his hand into a fist, clutching his brass knuckles, and slammed it into Ben's ribs. He immediately started gasping and wailing out in agony. Ignoring his cries,

Stitch growled, "A second piece of advice... Don't try to bullshit me. You lie, you pay."

"What do you want from me?"

"Last piece of advice." Stitch punched him again, causing the air to rush from Ben's lungs, "Don't make me repeat myself."

Ben wasn't a small guy. He was just over six-two and weighed about two-seventy, but it didn't matter how big or small the guy was. Brass knuckles to the ribs hurt like a motherfucker. It took him a moment to collect himself, but once he was able to catch his breath, Ben muttered, "I don't know how I got pulled into this. I was just supposed to show up in one of her classes and ask her out."

"And why were you supposed to do that?"

"So I could get closer to her and earn her trust."

I'd been struggling with the fact that Elsie's life had been in danger, and hearing Ben discuss the details of it made my stomach turn. I'd already heard from her what had happened. It didn't take much to piece the rest together. Bruton wanted his grandson to sweet talk Elsie into giving him information on the club, and when she didn't buy into his tricks, he panicked and tried to take her.

He'd threatened her life, and for that, I wanted to charge into that room and beat the hell out of him myself. The fact that I couldn't kill him, much less beat him, was eating at me. I could feel the tension building inside me. My palms were sweating, and my heart was racing. I wanted to hear everything the asshole had to say, but I was quickly reaching that point of no return.

I needed to step away and clear my head before I lost it.

I didn't like it, but I knew Stitch would get the information we needed. With that in mind, I turned to Torch and said, "I'm going to check in with Big."

He nodded, then said, "I'll keep you guys posted."

"Appreciate it, brother."

I took one last look at the two-way window and felt a twinge of satisfaction as I watched Stitch punch him once more. The guy deserved everything he got, so I felt zero remorse as I turned and walked out the door. As soon as I stepped outside, I tilted my head back, closed my eyes, and inhaled a deep breath of fresh air. I stood there for a moment, just taking in the night air.

It helped, but it wasn't enough to calm the storm that was raging inside my head. I opened my eyes, and the second I saw the sky full of stars, I knew the perfect place for me to get the reset I so desperately needed.

But first, I needed to check in with Big.

I took in one final breath, then made my way into the main clubhouse. I wasted no time and went directly to the office. When I walked in, I found him sitting at his desk with Maverick. As I approached, I could see that they were going over all of Bruton's financials and were trying to make some headway on the offshore accounts. "Having any luck?"

"Yeah, I think we're getting closer." Big glanced up at me, and the second he saw my face, he fussed, "Damn, brother. You look like hell."

"Been a long day."

"No sense in making it any longer. Go take a break." Big motioned his head towards Maverick. "We got this covered."

"I'm good. I've still got a couple of hours in me."

"We got it. Now, get the hell out of here and go check on your girl."

My first instinct was to argue and jump right into working with them, but deep down, I knew my head wasn't in the game, and I wouldn't be any help to either of them. I also liked the idea of checking in on Elsie, so I did as Big said and left them to it.

As I started out into the hall, I thought about Elsie and the shit day she'd had. I figured she could use a break from the crazy, too, so I went to the kitchen and grabbed a few drinks and a bag of her favorite chips. Once I had everything I thought we'd need, I made my way down to Elsie's room. My hands were full, so I had to knock with the tip of my boot.

It took her a minute, but eventually, the door eased

open and Elsie appeared with a surprised look on her face. "Whoa. What's all this?"

"Grab your coat. I have something I wanna show you."

"My coat?" Her brows furrowed. "Are we going somewhere?"

"Elsie, get it and come on."

"Okay, okay. I'm getting it." She reached behind the door and grabbed her coat. As she slipped it on, she asked, "Where are we going?"

"You'll see."

I handed her the bag of chips, then started down the hall. When we reached the roof access, I reached up and pulled the cable for the stairs. Once I had them down and in position, I started up the first step and said, "Come on."

To my surprise, Elsie didn't argue and followed me up to the roof.

When she reached the top, I took her hand and led her over to my secret spot. It wasn't anything special. It was just a couple of old chairs that were lit up by a strand of old Christmas lights, but it was quiet, and I knew no one would disturb us. When I plugged in the lights, a bright smile swept across Elsie's face. "This is so cool."

"I thought you might like it."

"I love it." As she sat down in one of the chairs, she

admitted, "I had no idea this was even up here."

"Most folks don't. That's why I like it up here."

I couldn't take my eyes off her as she tilted her head back and looked up at the stars. "Beautiful."

"Yes, you are."

"I was talking about the stars."

"And I was talking about you." I tilted my head back and rested it on the back of the chair. "Don't know how you do it."

"Do what?"

"Take a shit day and make it better without even trying."

"You do the exact same thing for me." She let out a sigh. "Today was awful. I just wanted to go to class and get what I needed for my project, and then Ben comes along and suddenly I'm wondering if I'm gonna get out of there alive."

"Really hate you had to go through that."

"I only have myself to blame." She looked over at me with puppy dog eyes. "But don't worry. Next time, I'll listen and do whatever you tell me to."

"You mean that?"

"Well, yeah. Of course, I do."

"Then, move in with me."

I knew it was fast. We'd only been dating for a couple of weeks, but I'd known for years that she was the one. I watched as her eyes widened and her mouth fell open, and when her nose wrinkled, I knew she was about to argue. "Move in with you? Seriously? We just started dating, and now, you want to live together?"

"Yeah, as a matter of fact, I do."

"You don't think that's rushing it a bit?"

"No."

"No?" She stood and started pacing in front of me. I knew then she was about to really amp it up. "We've been on two dates, and I'm not even sure that one of them was actually a date. I mean, we slept together, but we spent most of the night watching the game with the guys. I'm not sure that counts. But even it does, it's been two dates."

"It's been six years, Elsie. You know me better than anyone, and I'd dare say I know you just as well."

"Is that right?"

"Yeah, that's absolutely right." I stood up, and her face flushed red when I told her, "I know the only reason you like Oreos is because of the center. I know you like daisies because they remind you of your mother. I know you say you like scary movies, but you also sleep with a light on for days after watching one. I know you bite your bottom lip when you get nervous, and I know your cheeks flush whenever you see me come into a room, and they don't do that for anyone else but me."

A small grin slowly spread across her face as she

tucked a loose strand of her hair behind her ear, letting me know I was getting to her. "You definitely know how to win an argument."

"Only when it's important to me, and nothing's as important as you... You mean everything to me, Elsie." I brought my hands up to her face, gently brushing my thumb across her cheek as I said, "One look at you, and my day is made. I don't know a better way to say it than that."

"You said it pretty damn well." She studied me for a moment, then smiled. "Okay. I'll move in with you, but only on one condition."

"Let's hear it."

"I need you to not to forget about me."

"Hmmm? How could I forget about you?"

"Pretty easily actually," she scoffed. "When you're working on something, you tend to get tunnel vision. You go into your office, and there are times when you don't come out for days. I get it. I know you have things to do, and the brothers are counting on you for stuff, but I need you to find a way to fit me into the equation. Even if it's only for a few minutes."

"I can manage that."

"Okay, then I guess that settles it." She stepped over to me and wound her arms around my neck. "You should probably know... I'm not a very good cook."

"I'm aware."

"And I like cats, but I like dogs better."

"I know that, too."

"So, we're really doing this?"

I didn't answer.

Instead, I lowered my mouth to hers, kissing her with a promise of what was to come. The beat of her heart next to mine calmed me, refueled me, and that's when I knew. She wasn't my first, but she would be my *last*. I pulled her closer as I continued to devour her mouth, claiming her in the only way I could in that moment.

Damn.

I loved how her body instantly responded to mine, but it made it hard not to take her right there on the roof. I was quickly losing my restraint, so I stepped back and broke our embrace. Disappointment flashed through her eyes until I said, "I think it's time we took this inside."

She nodded, then waited as I unplugged the lights. We gathered the rest of our things and made our way back downstairs. I took her to my room, and we spent the next few hours tangled in each other's arms. A night with Elsie and a few hours of sleep were just what I needed to get my head straight.

The next morning, I woke up well before Elsie. I hated to leave her, but I was eager to find out what Stitch and Wrath had been able to get out of Ben.

Being careful not to disturb her, I eased out of bed, got dressed, and headed to Stitch's playroom. When I walked in, I found Savage and Two Bit standing at the two-way glass, and neither of them even noticed when I walked up.

I had no idea what had them so enthralled until I stepped up to the window. Ben was no longer hanging with his hands bound over his head. Instead, he was sitting down in a chair. He was drooped over, but I could still see that his face was bloody and swollen. It looked like he'd had a hell of a night. We were all staring straight ahead when I asked, "What's the latest?"

"He don't know shit," Savage grumbled. "Dude bribed him to take Elsie out, so he could get information out of her. But she wasn't having it."

"So, he didn't know anything about who Bruton had working for him?"

"Fuck no." Savage shook his head with disgust. "He thought it had something to do with the town council or some shit like that."

"You gotta be kidding me."

"Nah, this kid is as green as they come. Get this." He nudged me with his elbow. "He actually thought he had a chance with Elsie and got all butt hurt when she blew him off."

"Damn."

"Yeah, I almost feel bad for the guy."

I didn't hold the same sentiment as my brother, but I kept those thoughts to myself. I was about to ask him what Cotton thought about the situation when my phone chimed with a message. I got an uneasy feeling as I pulled my phone from my pocket. I glanced down at the screen, and as soon as I saw the message, I knew there was going to be trouble—big trouble.

Unknown Caller:
*** LET HIM GO***
*** OR THERE WILL BE CONSEQUENCES.***

CHAPTER 19
Elsie

I'd prayed.

I'd crossed my fingers.

I'd wished on falling stars.

But deep down, I never thought that things would work out for me. I thought I was destined to live a life full of disappointment and heartache. But last night, Wyatt proved me wrong. He asked me to move in with him, and for the first time in a very long time, I was excited about the future.

And I was looking forward to talking to him about it the following morning. Unfortunately, he disappeared again, and I was left wondering how long it would be before he returned. I curled up with his pillow and tried to go back to sleep, but I was too happy and excited, to even think about sleeping. I eventually gave up and got out of bed. I got dressed, then slipped down to my room to take a shower.

As soon as I was done, I got dressed and headed straight to Lacy's room. It was early. I was worried she might not be awake, but seconds after I knocked, her door opened, and she motioned me inside. "Hey."

"Morning." I stepped into her room and was surprised to find that it was in complete disarray. There were boxes scattered on the floor, and the clothes from her closet were piled on her bed. "Whoa. What's all this?"

"I'm packing up."

"What?"

"I'm leaving."

"You can't leave."

"I can, and I am."

"But why?"

"Because it's time for me to go." She ripped her favorite Aerosmith poster from her wall as she muttered, "If I'm being honest, I should've left a long time ago."

"What the hell are you talking about?"

"Seeing how happy you are with Wyatt has made me realize that I'm wasting my time here." She crumpled up the poster and shoved it in the trash. "I'm tired of being just a hang around. I just can't do it anymore."

"You're more than that." I walked over and sat down on the edge of her bed. "You're like family to everyone here."

"No, Elsie. I'm not." She reached up and pulled her Bad Company poster down from the wall. "I'm a club girl. I'm the one the guys wanna play with, but when it comes to picking an ol' lady, they always end up with a good girl like you."

"Why does that sound insulting?"

"You know I didn't mean it that way." She came over and sat down next to me. "It was great while it lasted, but it's time for me to face the fact that I'm never going to find my happily ever after unless I leave here."

"But what am I going to do without you?"

"I'm sure you'll manage just fine." She gave me a playful nudge. "Besides, you have Bones. I'm sure he will keep you entertained."

"Yeah, but it won't be the same."

"Maybe not, but it's for the best. You're an ol' lady now. It's time for you to start hanging with the other ol' ladies."

"You're serious about all this."

"Yeah, I am."

"But where will you go?"

"I'm not sure." She shrugged. "I might go stay with my grandmother for a little while. Save up a little money and maybe move down south. I don't know. I'll just see how it goes."

"When will you leave?"

"I'll wait until the lockdown is over, but after that, I've gotta go."

"I understand." I looked around at all the stuff she had to pack and asked, "Can I give you a hand?"

"No, it would be too depressing. Besides, you've got some socializing to do." She motioned her hand towards the door. "Darby and the girls are in the kitchen having breakfast. Time for you to go join them."

"You don't want me to help?"

"No, honestly, I need you to go." She grabbed a handful of clothes and stuffed them into a box. "Otherwise, I might end up changing my mind, and I really don't want to do that."

"Oh, Lacy."

"No. None of that." She shook her head and ushered me towards the door. "You gotta go."

I wanted to give her a big hug, but it was clear that she was in a fragile state. I didn't want to make things worse, so I smiled and said, "Okay, fine. Can I come back later? Maybe we can have a couple of drinks to celebrate your big move."

"Yeah, I'd be down for that."

"Good deal." I stepped out of the room as I told her, "I'll see you in a bit."

My heart was heavy as I turned and started down the hall. As much as I hated to see her go, I knew she was right to leave. She would never find what she was looking for at the clubhouse, but it broke my heart to think of losing such a dear friend. I knew we would promise to call and visit, and we would—for a little while.

But eventually, it would get harder and harder to keep in touch.

Time would get away from us, and before we knew it, a year or more would have gone by. While it saddened me to think of not talking to her every day, I couldn't help but feel excited for her. She was going after what she wanted, and with her stubborn streak, I had no doubt she would find it.

It was a thought that had me smiling as I walked into the kitchen, and it only grew wider when I saw that Lauren and Casey were sitting with Darby and the girls. I loved Lauren, but I hadn't seen much of her since she'd married Flynn. And it was the same with Casey. She'd been seeing some guy from school and rarely ever made it home. I rushed over to the table with a big smile and said, "Hey, guys! Long time no see!"

"We were just thinking the same about you!"

Lauren hopped up and gave me a big hug. "Where have you been hiding?"

"I've been around."

Casey stood and rushed over to me, hugging me tightly. "It seems like it's been ages since I've seen you."

"Because it has been ages. You never come home anymore," I fussed.

"Well, it's tough with school and all."

"I get it. I've been busy with school stuff myself."

"That's not all she's been busy with." A smirk crossed Darby's face as she teased, "From what I've heard, she's been pretty busy with our boy Bones, too."

"I heard the same!" Susana cocked her brow. "Spill it, lady."

"Well, we've been talking." I sat down next to Darby as I told them, "And it's been pretty great."

"I'm not surprised." Mia smiled. "I've always thought you two would be good together."

"We definitely have our moments." Normally, I would share the big news with Lacy first, but with her announcing her big move and all, I didn't get the chance to tell her about Wyatt asking me to move in with him. Not knowing how they'd take the news, I was a little hesitant to announce it to the girls, but before I realized what I was doing, I said, "He asked me to move in with him."

"What!" Lauren's mouth dropped. "Are you serious?"

"Yeah, we talked about it last night."

"So, you're gonna do it?"

"I am." I took a sip of coffee and smiled. "I mean, we'll have to wait until Cotton lifts the lockdown and all that, but..."

"That's awesome, Elsie." Lauren sounded sincerely happy for me. "Wyatt is lucky to have you."

"I'm just as lucky to have him."

We continued to banter back and forth, everyone sharing something about what was going on in their lives, and it wasn't long before the kitchen was roaring in laughter, especially when Darby and Susana started talking about how things were going at their school and how lame the college guys were. You couldn't miss the frustration in Susana's voice as she told us, "The last guy I went out with was a total asshat. He stayed on his phone the entire time and then got pissed when I told him I wanted to go home early."

"Oh, I hate when guys are so focused on their phones." Casey rolled her eyes. "I don't get it. Why bother asking us out if you don't plan to even try?"

"Exactly! It's like they are wasting both of our time."

"I'm over it." Darby threw her hands and huffed,

"I refuse to go out with another momma's boy with control issues."

"Oh, God. Don't get me started on the control issues," Casey grumbled. "I love Lewis, but if he doesn't stop pouting every time he doesn't get his way, I'm gonna lose it."

"Ugh. I hate that." Susana threw her head back with a groan. "I hate it even more when they try guilt-tripping you into doing stuff you don't wanna do, like going to their stupid frat parties or staying the night when you'd rather go home."

"What about when they try to check up on you all the time? It's like they're trying to catch you doing something." Darby giggled as she added, "Which I usually am."

"We're dating the wrong men," Mia announced. "Actually, men is the wrong word. We've been dating boys. Immature, spoiled-rotten boys. We need to be dating men."

"I agree." Susana shrugged. "But *men* are in short supply."

"Not around here." Mischief flashed through her eyes as Mia announced, "In fact, there is one that's caught my eye, and I'm thinking about starting something up with him."

"With whom?"

"Wrath?"

"Wrath?" Darby gasped. "Our Wrath?"

"The one and only."

"You've got to be kidding?"

"No, I'm not kidding. Not at all." Mia twirled a thick strand of her long, black hair around her finger. "I'm telling ya, I've dated the bankers, the lawyers, and the preppy college boys, and none of them have ever made me feel the way I do when that man looks at me."

"He's definitely hot, and he's got that whole intense thing going." Concern marked Susana's face as she asked, "But what about your dad?"

"What about him?"

"If he even thinks about getting involved with you, Stitch will kill him!"

"Dad loves Wrath."

"He likes Wrath. He loves you, and you know how protective he..." Darby stopped mid-sentence, then turned her head and started to sniff the air. "Do you smell that?"

The words had barely left her mouth when I caught the faint smell of smoke. "Yeah. Is something burning?"

"I don't know, but it certainly smells like it."

She and I got up and started trying to find the source of the smell, and it wasn't long before the others joined in. Seconds later, we heard a commotion outside and went over to the window to check things out. That's when we spotted a small fire in the back corner of the garage. "Holy shit."

Susana raced over to the back door and pushed it open as she shouted, "Fire!"

We all followed after her, and that's when we noticed that the garage wasn't the only thing on fire. Clutch's SUV and the front gate were also going up in flames. Two Bit and Savage each had fire extinguishers and were doing their best to tend to the fire at the front gate, while Hayes and Smokey were working on the one at the garage.

At first, it looked like no one was doing anything about Clutch's SUV, but then I spotted Rooster with the water hose. He tugged it over to the front of the truck and started spraying it with water, but instead of putting out the fire, it seemed to stoke the fire. The smoke was really starting to billow when Cotton and several of the brothers came barreling out of the clubhouse.

I had no idea how the fires got started, but it was clear they were intentional. It was mayhem, and it was absolutely terrifying.

The clubhouse was under attack.

I'd seen the guys wounded. I knew they'd been in fights before.

But never at the clubhouse.

Eager to put them out, the brothers scattered and started doing whatever they could to help. Darby was about to go give them a hand when Cotton spotted us and ordered, "Girls! Get back inside. Now!"

"But, Dad..."

"Get your ass inside, Darby!" Cotton roared. "And find your mom!"

That's all it took for all of us to go rushing back towards the back door. I was about to follow Mia back inside when I heard an odd buzzing sound above my head. I stopped, and when I looked up, I spotted a large, white drone suspended in the air above the clubhouse. I was trying to get a better look at it when Mia reached back and took hold of my arm, pulling me inside. "You better move it, or Cotton's gonna have your ass."

"Yeah, I'm coming."

I didn't have a good feeling as I followed her back inside.

Something big was going down, and I feared it might be the end of us all.

CHAPTER 20

Bones

The club had gone to great lengths to ensure our families' safety. We had nine-foot fences topped with barbed wire and multiple guards at the gate who were constantly watching and waiting for any potential attacks.

To discover that we'd been breached was alarming.

It was even more alarming to discover how we were breached. Bruton had used drones to drop incendiary devices throughout our compound. The devices were filled with thermite—a powder that creates a brief burst of heat and high temperature, but the flame is short-lived.

It was a smart move.

The drop was quick and effective, and it made a hell of an impression. It had us all scrambling. We had no idea what was coming next, and that had us all on edge. We were doing what we could to put out the fires when Cotton called Two Bit and Diesel over. "Go in and gather the others in the family room. Have them wait there until we figure out what the hell is going on."

"You got it."

They both headed inside, and I was about to go over and help Stitch and Rooster with Clutch's SUV when I heard my phone chime with a message. My entire body tensed as I reached into my back pocket and pulled out my phone. I looked down at the screen, and my blood ran cold when I read:

Unknown Caller:

Let him go.

*Or the next drop will be on the clubhouse, and **I will burn it to the ground.***

I immediately turned to Cotton and showed him the message. Needless to say, he wasn't pleased. "Fuck this guy."

Noting his anger, Maverick and Guardrail came over to see what was up. Cotton held up my phone, and as soon as he saw it, Maverick scoffed, "I say let him go. Hell, he's no good to us anyway."

"He's right," Guardrail agreed. "The kid doesn't know a damn thing. No sense in keeping him here."

"But what kind of message does that send." The vein in Cotton's neck pulsed as he growled, "I don't want this motherfucker thinking he can play us."

"I get that, but damn, Prez." Maverick sounded torn as he told him, "Our hands are tied on this one."

"Goddamn it. This motherfucker is gonna pay for this shit." Cotton shook his head and sighed. He lowered his head, thought for a moment, then inhaled a breath and said, "Let him go, but I want a tracking device on him—one that Bruton won't be able to find. That way, we can get the kid back if we need him."

"Shouldn't be a problem. Big and I can take care of it," I assured him. "Just need a few minutes to get it set up."

"Get it done."

I nodded, then followed Big inside. When we got to the office, Big took one of the smaller trackers from our safe and said, "This should do it."

It wasn't much bigger than a pen head and could easily be hidden anywhere. "Yeah, I should think so." He handed it to me, and I started prepping it. Once it was ready, I handed it back to him and said, "It's all set."

"Good. Let's get it to Cotton."

By the time we got to the playroom, Stitch and

Wrath had Ben cleaned up, but he still looked like hell. He was black and blue, and his eyes were swollen like he'd been in a boxing match and lost. They were in the process of giving him some clean clothes when Big walked into the room and grabbed his shoes, secretly slipping the tracker into the bottom sole. Once it was secure, he tossed them on the floor next to Ben's feet.

We all watched as he bent down to get them and groaned. The guy was in bad shape, which led Big to ask, "You think he's up to driving?"

"He's gonna have to be." Cotton gave him a once over and grimaced as he reached over and placed his palm on Ben's forehead, forcing his head back so he could get a better look. "Maverick can drive him into town. From there, he's on his own."

"I'll be fine. I can make it."

"We'll see soon enough."

"You should consider yourself lucky. Most folks don't leave here breathing. Best do what you can to steer clear because if there's a next time, you won't be so lucky."

"Don't have to worry about that. I have no intention of crossing paths with you guys again."

"For your sake, I hope you don't."

Ben put on his shoes, then followed Stitch and Cotton out to the parking lot. Ben was about to get into his car when Cotton stepped over to him and grabbed him by the shirt collar. He pulled him close as he growled, "Tell your grandfather I'm coming for him."

"I still don't understand what's going on with all this. Why do..."

"Just tell him."

Ben nodded, then got in the car. As soon as Maverick started the car, Cotton leaned down to the window and ordered, "Get him to the town square. He can get home on his own from there."

Maverick nodded, then drove through the gate and Two Bit followed close behind. As soon as they were out of sight, we headed back into the clubhouse. We gathered in the conference room and had just sat down when Cotton turned to me and ordered, "Message him back. Tell him we've released the kid."

"On it."

As I reached into my pocket, I was hit with a thought that had been weighing on me from the very beginning. I still didn't get why Bruton continued to message me instead of Prez or Stitch. Hell, he could've messaged any one of the brothers, and it would've made more sense than contacting me. Just thinking about it had me turning to Savage. "You said Ben didn't know anything, right?"

"Yeah, he was oblivious." Savage leaned back in his chair and toyed with his ballpoint pen. "Like I told ya before, he had no idea what Bruton was really up to and had no idea what he wanted from us. Just said that he wanted him to see what he could get from Elsie."

"So, it was a bust. He didn't get *anything* from her."

"Just the contact information on her phone, but Bruton already had our contact information."

"But he didn't have my burner number." I held up my phone. "He definitely has that now."

"That he does." He glanced down at the screen. "Did you message him?"

"Yeah, I sent it."

It wasn't until I glanced down at the screen that I noticed Bruton had responded.

Unknown Caller:

Smart move

I think it's time for us to meet.

You and your president, at my place tomorrow at 2.

Come alone.

"Shit." I took my phone and slid it over to Cotton. "He messaged again."

Cotton picked up the phone and looked down at

the screen, and as soon as he read the message, he ran his hand over his thick, gray beard and cursed, "Son of a bitch. This motherfucker's got balls telling me where to be and when."

"He asking for a meet?" Guardrail asked.

"Tomorrow at 2. He wants Bones and me to come to his place alone."

"Don't give a fuck what he wants," Stitch growled. "That shit's not gonna happen."

"We gotta find out what the hell this guy wants with us."

"Yeah, but not like this. It's too fucking dangerous."

"Then, we'll take protective measures." Cotton's tone grew fierce as he said, "He attacked the clubhouse. He put our women and children in harm's way, and there's no way in hell I'm gonna let him get away with that."

Tempers were high, so I had to tread lightly as I asked, "But what if today wasn't about an attack?"

"What else could it fucking be?"

"A message... A means to an end." I might've been way off base, but I truly believed it when I told him, "Up until today, he hasn't done anything to us that we haven't done to him. He got information on us. We have it on him. He roughed up Q and Rooster, and we worked over Ben. *Tit for tat.*

Might've stayed that way if Ben hadn't been his grandson."

"That's a bit of a stretch, don't ya think?"

"The fact that he not only used thermite, but also knew to use it should give us pause. So, no. I don't think it's a stretch. Today could've been a lot worse if Bruton wanted it to be."

"Maybe it's just me, but I don't give a fuck what it could've been. He fucking torched my SUV," Clutch roared. "I say we give this asshole a taste of his own medicine and burn his house to the fucking ground."

I wanted to argue and tell him that he was letting his anger get the best of him. Thankfully, I didn't have to say a word. Cotton said it for me. "We'll get him. You don't have to worry about that, but first, we need to find out what this fucker wants from us."

"You really think it's a good idea for you and Bones to go over there alone?"

"We aren't going there alone." Cotton turned to Maverick and Stitch as he said, "You boys are coming with us to make sure nothing goes down."

Stitch was quick to reply, "To do that, we're gonna have to find a position that's far enough away that he won't spot us but close enough where we can make a move if one is needed."

"Do what you gotta do. Just make it work."

"We'll get it covered." Maverick turned to Big as he

said, "We're gonna need eyes and ears on them when they're inside."

"I'll take care of it."

"We're also gonna need to get blueprints of the house and an aerial view of his property and of those nearby."

"On it."

Big pulled up his laptop, and it wasn't long before they were forging a plan that they hoped would keep Cotton and me out of harm's way. But I knew no such plan existed—not when you were dealing with a guy like Bruton. It seemed he was always one step ahead, and that had me concerned. I was still struggling with the fact he wanted me in on this meet.

It was one thing to send me messages.

It was another to want a face-to-face.

I couldn't help but think there was something he wanted from me, but I had no clue what that could be. It was something I couldn't stop fixating on. My brothers were hammering out plans and securing our safety while I sat in a complete daze, going through all the possible reasons for his interest in me.

I could remember seeing him in high school. I knew he was a history teacher. I never actually had him, but from what I'd heard, he was decent and fair. Only time would tell if that was still the case. Thankfully, the meet was just a day away, so I wouldn't have to wait much longer to find out.

The guys had been at it for hours. It was getting late, and everyone was growing both tired and irritable. Realizing that it was time for a break, Cotton announced, "It's time to call it a night. You boys get some rest, and we'll start back here first thing in the morning."

"I'm gonna say it again. I don't like any of this," Stitch announced. "I don't care what precautions we take. It's too fucking dangerous."

None of us knew how things were going to play out. Cotton and I could go there, and we could come to some kind of understanding with Bruton, or he could kill us on the spot. There was no way any of us could know for sure. Cotton knew as well as I did that we had to go, so I wasn't surprised when he replied, "It has to be done, brother."

"I don't know. I'm thinking Clutch had the right mindset," Stitch scoffed. "We should just burn his place to the ground and be done with this guy."

"It wouldn't be that simple, and you know it."

"Yeah, I know." Stitch turned to me as he said, "I just wanted my sentiments to be known."

"Understood." Cotton gave Stitch a pat on the shoulder as he assured him, "I'll keep a close eye on your boy."

"I plan to keep an eye on you both. We all do."

With that, Cotton dismissed the meeting, and the brothers called it a day and dispersed to their rooms. And I was more than ready to do the same. Even more so, I was ready to see Elsie.

It was selfish of me, but if there was even the slightest chance that things could go south, I had to let her know exactly how I felt about her. I needed her to know I loved her and wanted to spend the rest of my life with her. It was that thought that weighed on my heart as I headed to my room. When I opened my door, I expected to find her sleeping in my bed, but that wasn't the case.

The room was completely empty, and that had me charging out of my room and heading back down the hall. I'd been waiting all day to see Elsie, *all fucking day,* and I wasn't going to wait for a second longer. I charged down to her room, and without even knocking, I opened her door and stormed inside. I stepped over to her bed, and the second I pulled the comforter back, her eyes flashed open.

It took her a moment, but once she saw that it was me, Elsie gasped, "Wyatt! What are..."

Her mouth clamped shut when I leaned over her and quickly lifted her out of bed, cradling her in my arms. She didn't resist; instead, she slipped her arms around my neck and rested her head on my shoulder. Damn. That's all it took.

The tension I'd been carrying around began to lift from my shoulders. When we got to my room, I kicked the door shut and lowered her feet to the floor. I towered over her as I growled, "I thought we had an understanding."

Her eyebrows furrowed with confusion as she asked, "What understanding?"

"That you would move in with me."

"Okay, but you never said when you wanted that to happen."

"*I want it now.*" I stepped forward, pinning her against the wall. "I want you in my room, in my bed, from here on out. You think you can manage that?"

She nodded with a smile. "Yeah, I can manage that."

"Good."

I looked down at her and my chest tightened at how beautiful she was. She was perfect, every fucking inch of her, and she was mine.

Mine to cherish.

Mine to protect.

And I was going to do exactly that.

CHAPTER 21
Elsie

"I'm not gonna be around much tomorrow... I've got someplace I've gotta be."

"Oh, okay. Where do you have to be?"

"I can't get into it. I just needed you to know."

I could tell something was wrong. I could see it in his eyes, hear it in his voice. I couldn't help but wonder if it had something to do with the fires and the drones, but I didn't bother asking him. I knew he wouldn't tell me, but I got the feeling that he was going to be in danger and the thought of something happening to him ripped at me. Wyatt was my world, and I wanted nothing more than to plead with him not to go.

At the same time, I knew how much his club and brothers meant to him. Even though I wanted to, I couldn't ask him to walk away from his obligation to them. My voice trembled as I asked, "Should I be worried?"

He wrapped his arms around me and held me close to his chest as he whispered, "No, there's nothing to it."

He was lying.

Wyatt never lied.

He avoided things. He didn't tell me things.

But he never lied—not to me.

I knew then it was even worse than I thought and suddenly felt like someone had wrapped their hand around my throat. Tears started trickling down my cheek as I whispered, "*Wyatt*."

"Hey, now. None of that," he whispered as he wiped a tear from my cheek. "I won't be gone long."

"You promise?"

He didn't answer.

Instead, he lifted his hand to the nape of my neck, pulling my mouth to his. An eager moan echoed through the room when his tongue brushed against mine. With just a simple kiss, he sent a surge of heat coursing through my body, burning me to my very core and the world around us drifted away. It was just him and me. His rough palms slid effortlessly over my skin as he lifted my nightgown over my head and let it fall to the floor, leaving me standing before him in just my lace panties.

A rush of heat rolled against my skin as he stood there staring at me, appraising me. I'd never wanted anyone like I wanted him. I couldn't breathe, couldn't think, and the way his eyes filled with lust when he looked at me only made me want him even more. I reached out, grasped the hem of his t-shirt, and carefully pulled it over his head.

Once I'd tossed it next to my nightgown, I placed the palm of my hand on his chest and was relieved to feel that the beat of his heart was fast and hard like mine. "I don't know what's going on tomorrow, and I know you can't tell me. Just promise that you'll come back to me."

"Nothing could keep me away from you. I love you, Elsie."

It was the first time he said those words to me, so I let them resonate in my mind. I knew him well enough to know that I wouldn't hear them often. But right then, at that moment, it gave me something to hold onto. "I love you, too, Wyatt. With every single beat of my heart."

The words had barely left my mouth when his lips were back on mine. My breathing hitched when he gripped my sides and pulled me even closer. He trailed his lips down the side of my neck, sending shivers of pleasure surging through me, and it was all I could do to keep my knees from buckling beneath me.

My desire for him was running rampant through me, and I was losing what little control I had. Any inhibitions I might have had completely washed away when he took my bare breasts in his hands. He held them firmly while brushing his calloused thumbs across the sensitive flesh, and my head fell back as I arched my back. I loved the feel of his hands on my body—every touch had me longing for more.

I lowered my hands to his waist, quickly unbuckling his jeans. A hiss escaped his lips as I slipped my hand under the waistband of his boxers. Before going any further, I glanced up at him, and his eyes locked on mine as I delved deep into his boxers.

His breathing became short and strained as my fingers wrapped around his hardness. I could feel his pulse throbbing against my hand as I slowly started stroking him. I tightened my grip as I glided my fingers up and down. A feeling of satisfaction washed over me when his head fell back with a deep-seated groan, letting me know that I was giving him pleasure—the kind of pleasure he'd given me.

My confidence was growing by the second, and it wasn't long before I found myself grasping at his jeans. I lowered them down his hips, exposing his long, hard shaft. The next thing I knew, Wyatt had lifted me into his arms and was carrying me over to the bed. "Had all the teasing I can take. I need to be inside you."

The words had barely left his mouth when I was on the bed. He tugged his boots and socks off, then his jeans. With the weight of his body pressed against me, his mouth dropped to my ear, the warmth of his breath sending goosebumps down my spine as he whispered, "So damn perfect."

Wyatt's hands dropped to my hips as he slowly slipped my panties down my legs. A needy moan vibrated through his chest as he gazed down upon my naked body, then a devilish grin spread across his face while he settled his hips between my legs, making my entire body tremble. Lowering his face to my neck, the bristles of his day-old beard prickled against my skin as he nipped and sucked along the contours of my body.

A part of me wanted to go slow and savor the moment, but I was too far gone. I couldn't restrain myself. I wanted him. I needed him. Spreading my legs further to accommodate him, I shifted my hips up towards him as he raked his thick erection against my clit. My entire body ached for him.

"You ready for me?" he asked.

Unable to even string together coherent words, I nodded, praying that he wouldn't stop. I wound my hands around his neck, pulling him closer as I kissed him.

His hand slipped between us, and his fingers entered me. Each movement was meticulous and slow, causing me to writhe beneath him while his thumb brushed back and forth over my clit.

I was unable to control my whimpers of pleasure as he delved deeper inside me. I didn't recognize my own voice as it echoed through the room. I was completely lost in his touch, loving the feel of his calloused hands against my body. The bed creaked as I arched my back, feeling the muscles in my abdomen tighten with my impending release. My breath caught in my throat as waves of pleasure rushed through me, and just when I thought I couldn't take it a minute longer, his hand was gone. He reached for a condom, and once he'd slipped it on, Wyatt was back on top of me.

His forehead rested against mine as he grazed his cock against me. His erection, hot and hard, burned against my clit before he thrust deep inside, giving me all he had in one smooth stroke. I inhaled a quick breath, and Wyatt immediately froze. "You okay?"

"I'm more than okay." I lifted my hand to his face. "You don't have to hold back. I can take whatever you have to give."

I rocked my hips forward, begging him to continue. His hands reached up to the nape of my neck, fisting my hair as he drove into me again. Slow and demanding, he was in complete control. His teeth raked over my nipples, and I cried out wanting more. I dug my nails into his back as my whole body ignited with intense heat, unlike anything I'd experienced before.

Wyatt thrust deeper inside me, and as I tightened around him, he let out a growl and then quickened his pace. His control shattered, and unable to restrain himself any longer, he drove into me with hard, steady strokes. I fought to catch my breath as I felt my climax approaching. My entire body jolted and shook as my orgasm crashed through me.

I was still in the throes of my release when he found his own. Moments later, his body collapsed on top of mine, exhausted and sweaty. I loved the feeling of his body pressed against my bare skin, buried deep inside me. He took a moment to catch his breath, then tossed his condom and settled next to me on the bed. Neither of us spoke.

We just lay there, listening to the sounds of our breathing slow, and it wasn't long before the silence started getting to me. I remembered our earlier conversation and the concern in his eyes, and I could feel myself getting worked up again. I didn't want that to happen, so I asked, "What happens when I graduate?"

"What do you mean?"

"Are you okay with me getting a job?"

"You can do whatever you wanna do." He leaned over and kissed me on the forehead. "You can get a job or stay at home. Whatever you want."

"Do you have room at your place for me to have an office?"

"I'll make room, and if it doesn't suit your needs, we'll find another place."

"Don't be silly. I love your place."

"Well, it's our place now." He reached over and pulled me over to him. "We just gotta get your stuff moved over."

"That shouldn't take long," I scoffed. "I don't have much stuff. Just my clothes and a few pictures."

"Then, we'll get you more stuff. Whatever you need to make it feel like home."

"You're all I need. As long as you're there, it'll feel like home." I glanced up at him, and my heart swelled when I saw the emotion in his eyes. He loved me. There was no question about that. But I couldn't help but wonder if he saw the same future that I did which led me to ask, "What about kids?'

"What about 'em?"

"Do you want to have any?"

The words had barely left my mouth when the mood shifted. Wyatt looked up at the ceiling and let out a deep breath, becoming lost in his own world of thoughts. And from the look on his face, it wasn't positive thoughts that were twirling around in his head.

"I'd always seen myself having kids, but if you

don't want them, I'm fine with that. I don't need anyone but you."

"I don't want you giving up anything you want for me." He turned to face me as he confessed, "But I can't promise that he or she won't be like me."

"Oh, Wyatt." I eased up on the bed so I could look him in the eye. "You are a wonderful, beautiful man with a big heart and a great sense of humor. You're incredibly smart, loving, and compassionate. I would be over the moon thrilled to have a child just like you."

"You didn't know me when I was a kid. I was a real handful."

"All kids are. Some just need a little more love and support."

"I needed a swift kick in my ass," Wyatt scoffed.

"Whatever works." I leaned down and kissed him softly. "I'd be willing to do whatever I needed to for our kids."

"How many kids are we talking about?"

"Two?" I shrugged. "Maybe three."

"Oh, man. We're definitely gonna need a bigger house."

"And a backyard and maybe a barn."

"A barn?"

"Well, yeah. We'll have to have a place for the pony."

"Pony?" His brows furrowed. "We're gettin' a pony?"

"Um-hmm. And maybe a baby goat."

"Okay. Whatever you want." He slipped his arm around my waist and pulled me to his chest. "But just know it's gonna cost you."

"Oh really? What's it gonna cost me?"

"I don't know. The next thirty or forty years."

"Sounds like a good deal to me."

"That's good 'cause you're stuck with me."

I wound my arms around his neck and smiled. "I wouldn't have it any other way."

I lowered my mouth to his, kissing him tenderly, then lowered my head to his chest. We spent the next hour talking about our plans for the future, pretending that neither of us were thinking about the potential danger that loomed in the back of our thoughts.

Pretending was the only thing that got us through.

And those few hours would be something I would hold onto when I woke up alone the next morning.

CHAPTER 22
Bones

It was tough getting up and leaving Elsie sleeping in my bed. I wanted nothing more than to lay there for another hour and just soak her in, but I didn't have that luxury. The guys were busy getting everything ready for the meet, and I needed to give them a hand. Being careful not to disturb her, I eased out of bed and grabbed some clean clothes from my closet. I slipped into the bathroom, and after a quick shower, I got dressed and put on my boots.

I gave Elsie one last look, committing her beautiful face to my memory, then I gave her a quick kiss on the forehead and walked out. I was eager to join the others, but before I faced the chaos of the day, I needed coffee and a bite to eat. As I headed into the kitchen, I was planning to get in and get out, but as soon as I walked in, I heard my mother gasp, "Wyatt."

"Hey, Mom." I continued over to the coffee pot as I asked, "What are you doing up so early?"

"I couldn't sleep."

"Something wrong?"

"I don't know." Worry filled her eyes as she told me, "I've been with Griffin long enough to know when something's going on with the club, so I know something's up. But this time is different. This time, he seems more on edge than usual, and that makes me nervous."

"It's nothing, Mom."

"He said the same thing, but my motherly instincts are telling me otherwise. They're telling me that something's very, very wrong, and I've had to fight the urge to lock you in a closet."

"*Mom.*"

"I know. I know." She stood up and walked over to me, then wrapped her arms around me, hugging me tightly. "You just mean so much to me, and I don't want anything to happen to you."

"I'm fine." I hoped that I wasn't lying to her as I said, "Nothing's gonna happen to me. You're worrying for nothing."

"I certainly hope you are right." She gave me one last squeeze, then released me and rushed for the door. "Love you!"

"Right back at ya."

Our little encounter didn't make me feel any better about my future meet with Bruton. In fact, I couldn't have felt worse. I poured my coffee and grabbed a biscuit from the stove, then headed for the conference room. When I walked in, everyone was already gathered and busy hashing over the final details of the day. Stitch and Maverick were reviewing their maps with Smokey and Two Bit while Cotton and Guardrail spoke quietly in the back corner of the room.

I didn't see Big, so I slipped out and went to see if he was in the office.

When I walked in, I found him at his desk working on the camera and microphone that Cotton and I would wear when we entered the house. He was making sure the cameras were synced and working properly, and he didn't seem to notice I'd walked into the room until I sat down next to him. "Hey, brother. How ya holding up?"

"I've been better."

"This whole thing getting to ya?"

"You could say that."

"What's got you so twisted?"

"Every fucking thing." I leaned back in my seat. "I feel like everything's on the line, and it's up to me to make sure this whole thing doesn't blow up in our faces."

"It's not all on you, brother."

"It certainly feels that way." I shook my head. "It's been weighing on me so much I feel like I can't fucking breathe."

"It's not the weight of the load that will get ya. It's the way you carry it." He reached over and placed his hand on my shoulder. "This is one load you don't have to carry on your own. We're gonna be right there carrying it with you."

"Appreciate that, brother."

"Just telling it like it is." He lifted the camera he'd been working on as he said, "Now, quit your bellyaching and help me get this shit ready."

Big and I got the mics and cameras prepped, then carried them to the conference room. There, we ran through the entire plan with Stitch and Maverick, discussing where each of the brothers would be positioned during the meet.

Once we'd gone over every detail, we went out to the gun safe and gathered our artillery. We checked the rounds, then loaded everything up into the assigned SUVs. I got in the truck with Cotton, and with Stitch and the others following close behind, we drove over to Bruton's place.

On the way over, neither of us spoke.

We used the time to mentally prepare for whatever lay ahead—but neither of us could've prepared for what was coming.

When we pulled up, I was surprised to see that there were no guards, no crazy drones flying overhead or vicious dogs ready to attack. It was just a regular house with a black Honda Accord parked in the drive. Cotton killed the engine and announced, "We're here."

Maverick was quick to reply, "We're in position and have you covered. You're good to go."

While I was relieved to know that they were there and watching, I still had an uneasy feeling when Cotton turned to me and asked, "You ready?"

"As ready as I'll ever be."

He nodded, then opened his door and got out. I followed suit, and we both made our way up to the front door. Cotton knocked, and as we waited for Bruton to answer, I turned and looked around at all the rose bushes and potted plants. It didn't seem like we had the right place until the door eased open, and Bruton appeared.

I found it almost humorous that our mysterious adversary was wearing a pair of black slacks and a white button-down with a maroon sweater vest. His horn-rimmed glasses were perched high on his nose, and his thin, gray hair was neatly combed to the side, making him appear to be nothing more than your typical grandpa.

Like we were long-lost friends, he greeted us with a

warm smile and said, "Well, hello, boys. It's nice of you to stop by."

"Hello, Mr. Bruton." Cotton cocked his brow as he asked, "Or should we call you Davenport?"

"Bruton's fine. Just fine." He motioned us inside as he said, "Come on in and make yourselves comfortable."

Cotton was cautious as he stepped into the house. He took a quick look around, checking for any signs of potential danger, and once he felt the coast was clear, he gave me a nod, letting me know to follow. As soon as Bruton closed the door behind us, he grabbed a glass from the side table and stepped in front of us. "I think it's best that this conversation stays between us."

"I'm not following."

"Your listening devices. You won't be needing them." He raised the glass and gave it a slight shake. "Oh, and while you're at it, you can tell your friends that I'm unarmed. There's no need to keep a watchful eye. You both are in good hands."

His phony smile and friendly tone unnerved me, and I could tell Cotton felt the same when he looked over to me and removed his earpiece. He dropped it into the water, then they both waited for me to do the same. As soon as I lifted my hand to my ear, I heard Stitch say, "Just do it. We still have the chip in your belt and the camera. We got you."

I was reluctant, but I did as Bruton requested and took the earpiece from my ear. When I dropped it into the water, he smiled and said, "Good. Good. That's much better."

Bruton placed the glass back down on the table, then smiled and asked, "Can I get you fellas a drink?"

"Enough of the bullshit, Bruton," Cotton growled. "Just tell us what you want, and then, we'll be on our way."

"All in good time, son. All in good time." He motioned us over to a small sitting area as he said, "Come have a seat and let's get to know each other for a bit."

I could tell by his expression that Cotton had little desire to sit and chat with Mr. Bruton, but he did as Bruton requested. I walked over and sat down in the chair next to him, then waited for Bruton to finally tell us why we were there. He took a sip of his coffee, then turned his attention to me. "I've been looking forward to finally meeting you. You've been a true asset to your ah... *club*. I've been quite impressed with the work you've done."

"What work are you referring to?"

"All of it. You're an exceptional hacker. You've done things my people couldn't begin to do, and that's just the beginning. The success you've had playing the stock market has been extraordinary." Bruton looked to Cotton as he said, "You got lucky the day Stitch stumbled upon him."

"We get it," Cotton snarled. "You've done your research. And we've done ours."

"Of course you have. I wouldn't expect anything less." Bruton studied Cotton for a moment, then said, "And on that note, I would like to personally apologize for what occurred with your brothers, Q and Rooster. Orders were not followed, and the men responsible have been dealt with."

"They were dealt with? Is that supposed to fix things?" Cotton growled. "You've gotta be out of your goddamn mind! You not only got intel on my boys, but you got it on my wife and my kids. What the fuck is that!"

"I had to know who I would be going into business with." Bruton's face was void of expression. "I'm sure you can understand that."

"What does my daughters' class schedule tell you about me and my club?" I could feel the anger radiating off of him as he roared, "They have nothing to do with any of this!"

"What can I say? *I'm thorough.*" Bruton glanced over at me as he added, "I have no doubt that your intel on me is equally as thorough."

"And what about your stunt yesterday? Was torching my clubhouse part of your thoroughness?"

"I had to send that message. My grandson's life was in jeopardy."

"And what makes you think yours is not?" Cotton's voice was low and menacing as he snarled, "I could kill you right here and now."

"You could, but I'm just a cog in the machine." He shrugged. "You end me, and it'll only be a matter of time before someone steps up to take my place. And when they do, they'll come for you. But let's not dwell on the what-ifs. Let's discuss possibilities. My intent wasn't to go to war with you boys. I want to go into business with you."

"You gotta be fucking kidding me!"

"No, I'm quite serious... I believe we could make a great deal of money together."

"Oh, yeah?" Cotton scoffed. "And how would we do that?"

"You're aware of my connections, are you not?"

"I am very aware, but I don't see what they have to do with us."

"I've recently lost one of my best hackers, and as a result, there's been a disruption in my line of distribution. I would like you boys to help me settle that disruption."

"So, what is it that you want from us?" Cotton crossed his arms and cocked his brow. "Our guns?"

"That's exactly what I want." I was stunned. I'd

come to Bruton's thinking that he intended to go to war with the club, only to learn that he wanted to go into business with us. The whole thing seemed surreal. Cotton seemed equally as flabbergasted when he asked, "And why in the hell would we ever tie up with you?"

"Because I don't play favorites. *I don't take sides.* I deal with the highest bidder, and I learned a long time ago it's typically not a neighbor." Cotton sat back in his chair as he listened to Bruton say, "My shipments go abroad where they can afford to pay, and trust me when I say, they pay, and they pay well."

"We have our own distributor."

The club had worked with Nitro for as long as I could remember. We got him the goods, and he got them in the hands of our buyers—whoever they might be.

We never knew where the guns went. There was a peace in not knowing. We didn't have to think about the kid down the street or gangs in the city using our goods to kill one another. We simply got our cash and went about our way. If we worked with Bruton, we would know our weapons were going overseas to the highest bidder, and they would be used on their land—not ours.

Bruton seemed unfazed by Cotton's declaration when he replied, "Maybe so, but I can more than triple your profits. But let me be clear, it's not just your weapons that I'm interested in. I want Bones."

"Come again?"

"I want Bones on my team. I need his expertise to ensure that things with the venture continue to run smoothly."

And just like that, it all made sense. I'd spent hours wondering why he'd singled me out, but never once had I imagined that he wanted me to work for him. I glanced over at Cotton, and he looked positively livid as he barked, "No fucking way."

"I'm not asking for him to leave your club. He will still be at your full disposal. I simply need to know that I can call on him if things don't go as planned or if I need him to complete a particular job."

"You can't think that we would actually go for this. *That I* would go for this."

"Money talks, Cotton, and I am offering you and your boys a great deal of it.... Trust me when I say this is a once-in-a-lifetime opportunity."

Cotton still sounded skeptical when he asked, "And if we take a pass on this opportunity of yours?"

"Then, you take a pass." Bruton leaned forward, and he actually seemed genuine as he told us, "I'm not going to force you to go into this venture with me. You can leave here today, and we can both continue on with our lives as if this never happened."

"You really expect me to believe that?"

"Absolutely. I have nothing to gain by going to war with you boys. I simply want to continue building the business, and I know I can do that with you." The tension in the room started to lift as Bruton said, "And who knows. Maybe one day, the whole thing will be yours. You just have to be willing to take a chance."

Cotton took a moment to consider everything, then said, "This isn't a decision I can make here and now. I'll have to talk it over with the brothers."

"Of course. That's completely understandable."

Cotton stood as he asked, "When do you need an answer?"

"I'll give you until the end of the month." Bruton stood and stepped over to Cotton. He extended his hand as he said, "I do hope that you boys will consider my offer."

"We'll talk it over." Cotton shook his hand. "But I make no promises."

Bruton nodded, then turned his attention to me. "I do hope we get the opportunity to work together. The way your brain works is intriguing. I have no doubt that we could do great things together."

I didn't respond.

I simply gave him a quick nod, then followed Cotton out of the house. We went straight to the truck, and Cotton wasted no time starting the engine and getting the hell out of there. Once I was certain we were out of harm's way, I leaned my head back on the headrest and sighed, "That is not at all how I thought today would go."

"Not exactly what I expected either."

"So, are we really gonna consider this?"

"It's an interesting offer."

"Yeah, but he firebombed the clubhouse."

"Yes, he did, but I would've done the same to him if he had one of you."

"I get that."

But, like I told Bruton, this isn't just up to me. It will be up to the club to decide what we do, and if we do happen to go through with this thing, it'll be on our terms. *Not Bruton's.*" Knowing I'd be concerned, Cotton was quick to add, "But whatever we do, it will be the best thing for everyone involved, including you."

"I understand."

"I hope you do, because that patch on your back means something. You're part of the Fury family, and no one in this family stands alone." Cotton looked at me as he said, "We'll decide together if we're gonna partner with this guy or go to war with him. Either way, we will stand together."

I had no idea what the future held for me or for the club, but I found solace in knowing that no matter what lay ahead, I would have my brothers there with me. And with them at my side, I could face anything—including David Bruton.

And babies.

And ponies.

And goats.

And whatever the good Lord threw my way.

Epilogue
ONE YEAR LATER

Elsie

"Okay, sweet girl." I gave Chloe's car seat a tug, lifting it from the backseat harness. "Let's go say hi to your grandparents."

I draped a thin blanket over the car seat, hoping it would protect her from the cool, crisp air. I closed the door and started up the hill. It was a beautiful spring morning. The sun was shining, birds were chirping, and the flowers and trees were blooming. It was the perfect day to visit my parents and brother.

Once I made it up to their gravesite, I threw down a blanket and sat with Chloe at my side. I looked over at their headstones, and guilt washed over me when I saw the dried, dead flowers wilting in the vase. I quickly grabbed the fresh ones I'd brought and replaced them as I said, "Hey, guys. I'm sorry it's been so long since I stopped by, but as you can see, I've been a little busy."

I reached over and lifted Chloe's blanket, letting the sun shine down on her adorable face. "Believe it or not, our girl turned two months old today. She's still getting up several times a night, but I don't mind. I enjoy having those quiet moments with her. Besides, I know it won't last."

Chloe started fussing, so I reached inside her car seat and felt around for her pacifier. Once I found it, I slipped it back in her mouth and said, "I finally heard back from that headhunter I told you about. He wanted to know if I was interested in working at a marketing firm in Seattle. It pays incredibly well, and I would be part of a four-man team with my own office. It sounds amazing, but I'm not sure I want to take on a job like that when Chloe is so young."

"I'm sure you aren't surprised. It's just like me to spend all those long nights studying and writing those stupid papers just so I could turn down my dream job. I know it's crazy, but I know it's the right thing to do.'

I glanced over my shoulder, and a twinge of sadness washed over me as I looked at the empty parking lot. There was a time when I wouldn't be at my parents' gravesite for five minutes before Wyatt would come rolling up to check on me. So much had changed over the past year. It was like I was living a completely different life.

"Oh, I heard from Lacy the other day. She called to tell me that Aaron asked her to marry him, and she said yes! She's officially engaged! Can you believe that? I'm so happy for her! They've only been dating for a few months, but he seems crazy about her. And she's definitely crazy about him. They're planning to come up for a visit next month so they can meet Chloe, and I can't wait to see them."

Chloe started fussing again, so I reached into the car seat again and grabbed her pacifier. I quickly slipped it into her mouth as I said, "There you go, sweet pea."

I waited to make sure she was good, then draped the blanket back over the car seat. I was trying to think about what else I wanted to share with them when I heard the faint rumble of a motorcycle. A smile swept over my face as I turned and watched Wyatt pull into the parking lot.

Unlike the times before, he didn't wait for me to come back to the car. Instead, he got off his bike and started over to us. He was wearing his jeans and Satan's Fury cut, and he looked just as unbelievably handsome as the first day we met. As soon as he approached, I smiled and said, "I didn't think you were coming."

"I couldn't miss the chance to see my girls." He knelt down next to Chloe and peeked under the blanket as he asked, "How's she doing?"

"She's been wonderful, just like always."

"I'm not surprised." Concern crossed his eyes as he asked, "And what about you? Are you doing okay?"

"I'm good. I was just about to wrap up things here and head home."

"Want me to take her down to the car?"

"Yeah, that would be great." I leaned over and gave him a quick kiss. "I'll be there in a minute."

"Take your time."

I waited as Wyatt lifted Chloe's car seat and carried it down the hill. When he opened the door and started to put her inside, I whispered, "I've got it good, Momma. Really good. He loves me like Dad loved you, and I couldn't ask for more than that."

I stood and picked up my blanket. I shook it out, then said, "I'm not sure when I'll make it back by. Just know that you're always in my thoughts, and I love you all."

I walked back down to Wyatt and Chloe with a full heart and a smile on my face. I was officially a believer.

Dreams really do come true.

. . .

The End

More from the Satan's Fury MC- SG coming soon!!

(Questions about Bruton will be answered in Wrath's story.)

*Short excerpt from Q: Satan's Fury MC-SG after acknowledgments. Thanks for reading and be sure to sign up for my newsletter: https://lwilderbooks.us18.list-manage.com/subscribe?u=a2c4c211615b2d7b3dd46289a&id=7f8e916141

Acknowledgments

I am blessed to have so many wonderful people who are willing to give their time and effort to making my books the best they can be. Without them, I wouldn't be able to breathe life into my characters and share their stories with you. To the people I've listed below and so many others, I want to say thank you for taking this journey with me. Your support means the world to me, and I truly mean it when I say appreciate everything you do. I love you all!

PA: Natalie Weston
Editing/Proofing: Marie Peyton-Editor, Rose Holub-Proofer,
Promoting: Amy Jones, Veronica Ines Garcia,
BETAS/Early Readers: Tawyna Rae and Amanda Quiles
Street Team: All the wonderful members of Wilder's Women (You rock!)
Best Friend and biggest supporter: My mother (Love you to the moon and back.)

Excerpt of Q: Satan's Fury MC- SG

CHAPTER 1

Q

It had been just over twenty years since the day I started prospecting for Satan's Fury, and everything had changed.

My brothers were older and were sporting crow's feet and silvered hair. Their kids were now grown. Some had chosen to move on, while others had not only patched in but now had a significant role in the club. Prospects were now brothers, and more had been called to prove themselves worthy. Hell, even the clubhouse itself had changed and was now updated with fresh paint and new furniture.

Nothing was the same—nothing except me.

I was still just the same ol' Q. I wore the same jacket, drove the same damn bike, and I was still flying solo. I'd come close a couple of times, but I still hadn't claimed an ol' lady. A few years back, I'd thought

Cotton's oldest daughter was the one for me, but falling for the president's daughter turned out to be a bad idea. In fact, that shit blew up in my face.

Lauren wasn't interested in me. She never was. Her eyes had always been set on Flynn—the kid who lived across the street from Cotton's place. I should've seen it coming. They'd been close for as long as I could remember, but I refused to see it.

I didn't want to see it.

Not that it mattered.

Lauren was crazy about the guy, and they'd been together for almost five years now. They were even talking about starting a family, and that was a hard pill to swallow—especially when I'd always wanted a family of my own.

I was stuck, like a damn stone planted in the middle of a river. Everything seemed to rush past me while I remained rooted in place. I couldn't help but wonder when I would finally break free, and those rapid waters would carry me along with them. Sadly, that day hadn't come.

And as I sat there at the clubhouse bar with Big and Clutch, I feared it never would.

After a long week, we'd all come to the bar to blow off steam. I'd just taken a pull from my second beer when Stitch and Maverick came over. I couldn't help but notice that Stitch looked absolutely pissed as they both sat down next to us. He reached for a beer as he grumbled, "I'm gonna fucking kill him."

"I know you want to, but you can't kill him, brother." Maverick chuckled under his breath as he added, "He's just a kid."

"He's no fucking kid. The asshole's almost twenty-five."

Stitch was the club's enforcer—a position he'd held since the day I'd patched in, and rightly so. The man was still a force to be reckoned with. When he had one of our adversaries in his chambers, he would bring the wrath of hell down on them, making them wish they'd never attempted to go up against the Fury brothers. Maverick's smirk remained intact as he goaded, "Yeah, he's twenty-five, and he's dating your daughter."

"That's exactly why I'm gonna kill him." Stitch's eyes grew narrow as he growled, "The asshole's been fucking with her head, and I'm not having it."

"Fucking with her?" All the brothers were fond of Mia. She was a smart girl, beautiful, with a good head on her shoulders, and she had a heart of gold, just like her mother. The thought of someone giving her a hard time drew me to ask, "What the fuck is this guy doing?"

"The motherfucker's up her ass all during the week, but when the weekend rolls around, he goes

MIA." Stitch grumbled curses under his breath before adding, "He's always giving her some fucking excuse like he had to work or had some family emergency, but you know as well as I do it's bullshit."

"Sounds like it... You really think he's messing around on her?"

"Fuck if I know, but it certainly looks that way."

"*Yeah, I'm afraid it does.* I'd be a hundred shades of pissed if some guy was pulling that shit with Lexie." Like Stitch, Maverick was extremely protective of his daughter, so I wasn't surprised when he nodded his head in my direction and asked, "You want me and Q to check this guy out and see if he's really fucking around?"

The words had barely left Maverick's mouth when Bones came up behind us. He was no longer the quiet, little Wyatt who'd kept his face buried in his electronics. Now, he was six-two and built like a linebacker, and he had no problem saying whatever was on his mind. His brows furrowed as he asked Stitch, "See if who's fucking around?"

"Nobody," Stitch grumbled under his breath.

Bones was Stitch's stepson, and even though they were polar opposites, the two were inseparable. It didn't matter to either of them that they weren't blood and had nothing in common. Stitch was his father—through and through, and they were as tight as a father and son could be. Knowing how close the two were, none of us were surprised when Bones gave him hell about being pissed. "Please tell me you aren't still bitching about that Tucker guy."

"That Tucker guy is..."

"An asshole," Bones interrupted. "Yeah, I know. You've said it a hundred times, but that doesn't change the fact that there's nothing we can do about it."

"I can cut off his balls and shove them down his fucking throat."

"Yeah, you could do that." Bones gave Stitch one of his looks as he replied, "But Mia would never forgive you for it, and you know you don't want that."

"Yeah, well, she'd get over it."

"Maybe. Maybe not." Bones took a slug off his beer, then suggested, "You could always let Maverick and Q follow him around a while and see what he's up to. For that matter, I could do a little digging of my own."

Big was the club's hacker, and he'd always been phenomenal at his job. He was usually the one who did the digging, but Bones had skills of his own. He was one of those guys who just knew shit—all kinds of shit, and he'd been like that since he was a kid. Some said it was the Asperger's that made him so astute, but I'd never bought into that.

The kid was just smart.

Plain and simple.

Hell, it was the reason we'd given him the road name Bones. He had skills like no other, and if there was digging to do, we all knew he could do it without question. I wasn't surprised when Stitch nodded and said, "Yeah, that sounds good. I'll be interested to see what you can find out about the douchebag."

"Me, too."

Bones turned and was about to head out when Elsie's head plowed into the center of his chest, causing both to stop with a jolt. Elsie stumbled back, then looked up at Bones with bright red cheeks. "Oh, crap. I'm sorry about that, Wyatt."

"No problem."

Bones seemed completely unfazed by their little exchange as he made his way towards the door. Elsie, on the other hand, was still sporting her blushed cheeks—which grew even redder when she realized we were all staring at her.

I gave her a playful wink, then said, "Hey there, Elsie girl. How ya making it?"

"Okay, I guess."

"What about your classes?"

"They're okay." The red in her cheeks started to fade as she announced, "I ended up making an A on that big paper."

"That's awesome."

EXCERPT OF Q: SATAN'S FURY MC- SG

It had been just over a year since the day Two Bit and I found her dumpster-diving at Danver's Sports Grill.

We'd gone out for a bite to eat with Cotton and a couple of the other brothers. We had a round of beers and a couple of burgers, and when Clutch ordered us a second round, Two Bit and I decided to step out for a quick smoke. We'd barely lit up before we heard a strange noise coming from one of the dumpsters. Curiosity got the best of us, so we went to check it out.

That's when we discovered a young girl bent over the side door of the dumpster, rummaging around for something to eat. As soon as she realized we'd come up behind her, she dropped whatever was in her hand and just stood there staring at us with an embarrassed expression.

The poor kid was filthy from head to toe and looked like she hadn't had a decent meal in weeks. Doing his best not to embarrass her even more, Two Bit gave her one of his charming smiles and asked, "Hey, kid. You alright?"

"Yeah, I'm good."

"You sure?" Two Bit motioned his head toward the dumpster. "'Cause it doesn't look that way."

"Yeah, I'm fine." Her eyes dropped to the ground with embarrassment. "I was... ah, just looking for my keys."

"Is that right?" Two Bit and I are big guys, and we

were both wearing our cuts and boots—which only made us appear more threatening, especially for a young girl like her. But surprisingly enough, she didn't seem intimidated in the least. She stood tall and maintained eye contact as I asked, "You got a name?"

"Yeah, I'm um... Sabrina."

"Sabrina, huh?" *I could tell she was lying, but I didn't push her on it. Instead, I asked,* "Your folks around?"

"Yeah, they're at home."

And another lie.

"So, if we were to take you home..."

Her eyes widened, and a slight gasp slipped through her teeth as she replied, "You can't do that."

"Oh, yeah? Why not?"

"Because they're..." *Her voice trailed off.* "You just can't."

"That's what I thought. You got any idea where they are?"

"Look, I'm sorry if I did something wrong here. Like I said, I was just looking for my keys. I didn't mean any harm."

"You're not in any trouble, kid," *Two Bit tried to reassure her.* "We're just trying to make sure you're okay."

"I told you. I'm fine."

"Yeah, you did." *Two Bit glanced over at me, then*

looked back to her. He studied her for a moment, then added, "But I'm not buying it."

Her brows furrowed as she snapped, "Sounds like a personal problem to me."

"We're just trying to help."

"I didn't ask for your help."

"No, you didn't." My throat tightened as I told her, "But I've been in your shoes. I know how hard it can be."

"You don't know anything about me or what I've been through!" She rolled her eyes, then started to walk off as she grumbled, "Just leave me alone."

She didn't get far when Cotton stepped in front of her, stopping her dead in her tracks. He looked down at her with concern as he asked, "What's going on here?"

"Nothing." She nervously bit her bottom lip as she looked up at Cotton and announced, "I was just leaving."

When Cotton turned to us, Two Bit was quick to explain, "We just found her going through the dumpster."

"I already told both of them..." the girl whipped back around, "I was looking for my keys."

"Oh?" Cotton studied her for a moment, then asked, "And how did they end up there?"

She didn't answer.

She simply stood there and glared at him.

"You got a place to go, kid?"

"Why do you care?" She glanced over at me and Two Bit as she asked, "Why do any of you care?"

"Cause it's thirty degrees out here, and you got no coat," I clipped. "We're not leaving you out here alone."

"Please just leave it." Tears filled her eyes as she told us, "I just gotta make it a couple more months."

"What happens then?"

"I'll be eighteen." Her eyes were filled with determination as she told us, "I won't have to be put in the system and end up in some place I don't wanna be."

"The way I see it, you got two choices." Cotton crossed his arms. "You can either come with us, or we're calling the cops."

"Why would I come with you?"

"We'll get you cleaned up and some real food in your belly." Cotton's expression softened as he told her, "And a warm place to lay your head. How does that sound?"

"It sounds great, but what's it gonna cost me?"

"Nothing, kid. Not a damn thing."

She mulled it over for a moment but eventually agreed to come with us.

After we got her some food, we took her down to one of the guest rooms where she took a shower, and then the girls got her some clean clothes and other girlie shit. It took a few days, but she finally opened up and admitted that she'd recently lost both of her parents in a house fire. She'd heard horror stories about the foster care system, so she decided to try and hide out until she turned eighteen. She left the only home she'd ever known and spent the next month living in her parents' car.

Our president was known to have a bit of a soft spot for folks like Elsie, who were having a hard time, so none of us were surprised when Cotton offered to make her stay more permanent. It only took a couple of months for her to settle in and become like family, and I was pleased to hear she was doing well in her college classes. "Proud of ya, kid."

"Thanks, Q." She rolled her eyes with a groan as she said, "The professor didn't make it easy. The guy's a grade-A asshole with a receding hairline and a bad case of halitosis, and he's intent on making my life hell."

"Sounds like a real charmer."

"Oh, he definitely is, but I won't let him get the best of me."

"That's what we wanted to hear." Clutch gave her a proud smile as he asked, "You up for taking a break from all the ball-bustin' tomorrow?"

"Yeah, I could use a break. What do you have in mind?"

"Some of us are heading out to Smokey's place tomorrow. Gonna do some grilling and help them set up for Pioneer Day."

I could still remember the day Smokey's dad died and left Smokey their family orchard. Smokey and his father weren't exactly close, so it was understandable that Smokey wasn't exactly thrilled about the idea. We all expected him to back out and sell the place, but MJ, his ol' lady, convinced him to hold onto the place. It took some time, but they'd completely revamped the entire place. It was no longer a simple apple orchard but a place for apple picking, gift buying, weddings, and family events.

It had become a local attraction that brought tourists in from all over, and they were expecting a huge turnout for their upcoming Pioneer Day. They'd have folks dressed up in pioneer clothes making jams and shit like they did back in the day, and there would be tons of activities for the kids. It was something we'd all come to enjoy, so I wasn't surprised when Clutch told Elsie, "I thought you might like to tag along."

"I'd love to."

"Good deal. We'll head out around nine."

"Sounds great." She glanced over at the clock, then told us, "Well, I should probably go get some studying done. You guys have a good night."

"We're gonna try."

Elsie gave me a quick nod, then made her way out of the bar. Once she was gone, I turned my focus back to my beer. I sat there quietly listening as Maverick and

Stitch bantered back and forth about their ol' ladies and the house projects they'd been working on. Neither of them sounded all that pleased about the extra workload that had been put on their plates, but I knew better.

They were both crazy about their better halves and would do anything to make them happy—even if that meant doing house renovations neither of them felt were necessary. I envied that about both of them. Hell, I envied that about all my brothers with ol' ladies, but I wasn't going to dwell on it.

Not tonight—which is why I got myself another drink.

And then, another.

And it wasn't long before the thought was nothing more than a distant memory.

Printed in Great Britain
by Amazon